Holding On and Letting Go

K.A. Coleman

LODESTONE BOOKS

Winchester, UK
Washington, USA

First published by Lodestone Books, 2014
Lodestone Books is an imprint of John Hunt Publishing Ltd., Laurel House, Station Approach, Alresford, Hants, SO24 9JH, UK
office1@jhpbooks.net
www.johnhuntpublishing.com

For distributor details and how to order please visit the 'Ordering' section on our website.

ISBN: 978 1 78279 577 3

A CIP catalogue record for this book is available from the British Library.

Design: Lee Nash

Printed in the USA by Edwards Brothers Malloy

Holding On and Letting Go

CONTENTS

To my parents,
Every great story needs a beginning,
And my journey started with the two of you.
I love you both.

Emerson

Some girls dream of their wedding: the perfect dress, the perfect husband, and the perfect dance. I guess I was shortsighted because I'd never thought about it that much growing up. Even as a seven-year-old, my dream was more realistic: high school. I knew I would get to high school someday, and the plan didn't hinge on Prince Charming proposing to me. I couldn't wait to be a high school student. In my head, I had all of these plans. I would take a photography class, run varsity track, learn a new language, build my friendships, volunteer, and run for Student Council. I knew exactly who I would be, and I was excited to become that person. That saying about the best-laid plans going awry? I think Steinbeck was underestimating how screwed up plans could become. My plans? They shriveled up and died.

As I sat in my older brother's car waiting for him to drive me to the high school that had once been my dream, I glanced in the mirror. My blonde hair was pulled back into a messy bun. Not a strategically messy bun that is actually well planned with the right amount of mess, but an actually messy bun because I just didn't give a crap about my hair. It didn't really matter. The blue eyes that stared back at me were dull. I used to love my eyes, but it's really hard to like your eyes when you hate the person staring back at you. I looked away from the mirror. I had seen enough for today.

My brother swung open the car door and glanced down at me skeptically. "Are you sure you want to wear that today?"

"I checked the handbook; there isn't a rule about skirt length," I replied while I eyed my severely short skirt wearily. The electric blue skirt served a purpose. If people were staring at my legs, maybe I could get through the day without anyone paying attention to anything else about me.

"Just checking," Brad remarked as he buckled his seatbelt.

I could have easily walked to school or driven my own car. The high school was only a few blocks from our house, but I didn't want to rain on my brother's guardian parade. Plus, I knew he just wanted to make sure I got to school, and there wouldn't be many chances for him to drive me. Recently, he had begun his residency in anesthesiology at a hospital in our town. Those hours would keep him busy, and I appreciated that he specifically applied to programs just around where we lived so that I could live with him. My older brother was certainly the best thing about the situation.

"Are you ready, Em?" Brad asked, interrupting my thoughts.

"Well, basically we bought out the school supply store last night, so I think that's as ready as I can be." I didn't really do well answering serious questions. If I could deflect with sarcasm, I deflected. It was easier that way

"You know what I meant," he chided.

Of course, I knew what he meant. Was I ready to see classmates who may or may not remember me? Was I ready to deal with questions about my two long years stuck in France with parents whom I actively hated? Was I ready to get the looks of sympathy from those who did remember why I landed in France in the first place? I didn't think I would ever be ready to deal with those things, but "being ready" had nothing to do with having to do it. With a big breath, I answered my older brother honestly this time. "I know I'm ahead academically, so switching in shouldn't be a problem. As for everything else, I'll just deal with it as it comes." I tried to sound more sure of myself than I was when I answered. There was no need for two of us to be nervous; my stomach was knotted enough for two anyway.

As my brother pulled into the parking lot that I had once dreamed of, it seemed silly that I would have set my sights on something so ridiculously dumb. What I should have been worried about was right under my nose the entire time, and I hadn't noticed it. I should have noticed it. I really should have noticed it.

Matt

"So what are we doing this weekend?" Savannah asked as she ate her yogurt. With every spoonful, she managed to flip her brown hair naturally. At least, I thought it was natural or otherwise she would have one hell of a crick in her neck after every meal.

Her best friend, Eliza, sighed as she thought about it. "I guess we could hit up the football game and party afterward."

When Savannah asked about plans, it usually meant she already had something in mind. I had been dating her long enough to know that she was never without a plan. For the most part, I didn't mind. It meant less work for me trying to come up with a date that probably wasn't satisfactory enough for her anyway. Savannah wasn't a bad person, but her parents had raised her with certain expectations and even she realized that. Her parents probably wanted her to be a debutante, but we lived a few states too far north and they were a few decades too late.

"Actually, I was thinking about something else." Savannah drew out her idea to up the drama. Like I said, I'd been dating her for a while. "My parents are going out for the night which means a hot tub with no parental figures anywhere in sight."

"Count me in," Luke spoke up immediately. He was my best friend and Eliza was currently his flavor of the month. "Are swimsuits optional?"

Eliza swatted at him and giggled flirtatiously. "Does it matter? My bikini leaves very little to the imagination." She winked at him smoothly, or at least what she thought was smoothly. I knew my friend though; Eliza was a flavor of the month for Luke. The quicker she realized that, the easier it would be on everyone.

"So it's settled, then?" Savannah asked with a smile on her face that said she knew the matter had been settled the second she brought it up. "Matt?"

"Yeah, babe, I'm in," I replied, sitting back in my chair and tossing an arm on the back of Savannah's chair. I was prepared to tune out the rest of the conversation between Eliza and Savannah. I didn't really get how two girls who saw each other every day and talked hourly could have so much to say to each other, but I'd come to accept it.

"Hey, Matt?" Luke's voice drew me out of my reverie.

"Huh?" I asked as I popped a handful of chips in my mouth.

"Is Emerson back in town?" Luke asked, staring off over my shoulder.

I almost coughed up my chips at the question. I hadn't seen or heard from Emerson in over two years. It seemed impossible that she would just pop back up out of nowhere.

"Who is Emerson?" Savannah asked, looking around to see whom Luke could be talking about.

"Matt's next door neighbor and best friend for over ten years," Luke replied, straining to see through the now heavier crowd.

Looking pissed, Savannah asked, "Why haven't I met her if she's so important?" Savannah's tone made it clear she was now very interested in meeting her and probably not to be her best friend.

As I continued to choke on my chips, Luke answered for me. "Because she's been living in France for the past two years or so. She went to elementary and middle school with Matt and me."

When the crowd finally parted a bit, I could see her. Emerson Kenzi Caulfield. She looked so much different since the last time I saw her, but I hadn't seen her since the end of eighth grade and we were juniors now. As I couldn't help but stare at the friend who had once been my world, I noticed that Emmy had probably grown a solid four inches since the last time I saw her. Clearly, she had finally inherited the Caulfield height and some slight curves; despite the weariness to her face, she was as strikingly beautiful as ever. Her high cheekbones and pouty little mouth remained firmly intact. When we were younger, Emmy always hated her mouth because she thought it made her look snobby. It never mattered though because of how much she laughed; her mouth had little time to take on a pouty expression. As I looked at her now, I didn't see the laugh that always made me smile back at her, nor did I see the mischievous light that normally emanated from her eyes. As a few people stopped to greet her, she gave each of them a half-hearted hug which was also new to me. Emmy didn't do anything half-hearted; she believed in bear hugs.

While I was stuck staring at a girl I had given up hope on, I noticed Luke leave the table to go greet her. Tripping over my chair, I followed in Luke's footsteps.

"Emerson," Luke bellowed cheerfully. "Welcome home, kid." He picked her up, wrapped her in a huge bear hug and swung her long legs around. Her already tiny skirt rode dangerously higher on her thighs. Yes, I was staring at her legs. Christ, they were long and tanned.

When Luke finally dropped her, she gave him a small smile. "Thanks, Lucas. I'm glad to be back."

As I stepped in closer to hug her as well, Savannah shot in front of me before I could react. Like a lion sizing up its prey, she leaned back against me. "And who are you?" she asked despite the fact that Luke had just told her exactly who she was only moments before. I watched Savannah eye Emmy from head to toe. Unfortunately for her, she wasn't going to find much wrong with Emmy in the looks department.

Emmy looked slightly bemused by the tiny brunette standing in front of her making demands. "Emerson," she replied after a minute. She glanced between Savannah and me a few times. Inside, I willed myself to say something, but it was as if I had literally swallowed my tongue.

Savannah hadn't lost hers though. Without being prompted, she introduced herself. "I'm Savannah Hayward. I'm on varsity cheer, and I'm Matt's girlfriend." She grinned up at me pleased with herself. Savannah didn't realize that being a Hayward and a cheerleader would have no impact on her current target audience.

"Cute," Emerson replied with a slight roll of her eyes. "I'm out of here." With that, she pivoted past Savannah, gave Luke a slight slug in the shoulder, and walked back toward the high school building.

"What an ugly bitch," Savannah said loudly enough that everyone standing in the nearby area watching our exchange could hear it.

I finally found my tongue and replied just as loudly as Savannah. "Watch it!"

Her eyes filled with frustration and she stomped back to Eliza in a huff. Eliza hadn't bothered to get up for the little show we put on for the rest of the student body eating lunch outside.

"I think that went exceedingly well," Luke remarked, glancing between me and the building.

"Screw you, Luke," I replied as I too watched the building. Two minutes ago, Emerson had stood only a foot in front of me, and I hadn't said one damn word. She and I had our own language when we were six for God's sake. How the hell couldn't I get one word out to her?

"You didn't know you'd see her today," Luke said with far less sarcasm in his voice. "You didn't know she was coming back. Give yourself a break, man, she caught you off guard."

He was right. I didn't know she was coming back. Hell, I didn't know if she was ever coming back. And she didn't just catch me off guard; she single handedly turned me upside down without ever speaking to me.

Emerson

School pretty much went how I expected. Gratefully, a lot of people in the few classes I attended that day didn't know me, so I didn't have to talk to them. Fortunately, I could handle silence. I got sized up like a piece of meat by a bunch of guys. The skirt did its job as intended. Only a few people stopped me to talk. Unfortunately, I didn't want to talk to them. It's not all that fun watching people who were once your friends handle you like you might shatter. The idiots didn't even get it. I passed shattered a long time ago; there was nothing left in me to break.

Luke didn't treat me as a breakable piece of fine china, which I appreciated. Then again, he could meet a queen, and he probably wouldn't bow down to her either. Luke and I became friends through Matty whom I'd known literally since birth. For the first ten years of my life, Matty really harped on the fact that he was indeed two months and one day older than me. When Matty became friends with Luke, I came as part of the package deal. Looking back, I suspect he thought we would hate each other, but we both loved Matty and that was all we really needed to have in common. I had thought about Matty a lot in the two years I spent in Europe; he contacted me a few times. I thought it would be easier to break our friendship completely, so I never returned his messages. Plus, I didn't have all that much to give as a friend anymore. They were both better off without me even if Savannah seemed like an annoying mosquito that I kind of wanted to swat. Today wasn't really about any of them anyway. They were minor obstacles on my way to my real destination.

As agreed, my brother wasn't picking me up from school today. I needed to do the next part of my day alone. After school, I walked three blocks in the opposite direction of where I lived. As I got closer to the location, I looked out over the grassy hills and fields. I didn't know if it made me feel better or worse that a place like this could look so pretty. From a distance, the sporadic flowers and wayward paths looked like something out of a painting. As I continued to walk though, I was very aware of what was under my feet: dead, decaying bodies and bones. There wasn't anything pretty about that picture. In fact, I wanted to run away, but I had already done that with my parents who were still running. I needed to stand still for a while.

As I approached the grave, I knelt down and touched the head stone. "Peter Ericson Caulfield. 2003–2010. Beloved little brother and fearless fisherman." Brad and I had designed the headstone and picked the words, but today was only the second time I was seeing them. I reached into my bag and pulled out a fisherman's hat and draped it on the cornerstone.

"Hi, Peter Rabbit," my voice cracked for the first time today, but I kept talking. I needed my little brother to hear me. "I know you hate that nickname, but I loved that story as a kid and when I first saw you in the hospital, you became my new love. You still are, Peter. I bought you a fisherman's hat that I thought you might like. I haven't been fishing without you. It wouldn't compare anyway; my favorite part of fishing with you was that you truly believed a shark attack was possible at all times, even when we were in a lake or standing on the ground. Maybe I should have explained the rules about sharks to you, but it was more fun the way you fished. You made the most boring hobby in the world a perilous adventure." I stopped for a second knowing that I hadn't come to talk about fishing and I was just stalling. "I'm so sorry it has taken me so long to get back here to you. I never wanted to get on that plane to France and leave you. If I could build a fort next to you here and live, I would do it." I wiped my eyes on the sleeve of my shirt. "Some days, I think it's still a terrible nightmare. You shouldn't be gone. It's not fair; the rest of us are older and you had so much ahead of you. It's a Catch-22, right? I can't believe there is a God so selfish that he would steal you from us when I need you so desperately, but I have to believe there is a God and you are in a better place because I couldn't keep breathing in and out if I didn't believe it. I was supposed to go first and come back to haunt you as a friendly ghost. God Pete, I never thought it would be the other way around." I gasped for air now. "I should have seen it coming. I spent the most time with you. The second you complained that you were too sleepy to come play soccer with me, I should have known to take you to the hospital and knew that something was really wrong. I'm sorry, Peter. I'm so, so sorry."

I allowed myself to collapse on my brother's grave sobbing. Every part of me ached with missing Peter and regret that I hadn't been able to stop the illness. I cried until I didn't have anything left.

Matt

After school, I drove straight to Emerson's house. Even though I knew skipping soccer practice would bench me for Saturday and mean miles of running, I had to get to her and actually form words this time. If I was lucky, I'd get out full sentences that actually made sense. I had hoped to catch her by herself during the afternoon, but we didn't have any classes together. And I knew better than anyone that Emmy was a master at hiding when she didn't want to be found.

When I pulled into her driveway, I once again tripped climbing out of my jeep. I could dribble a soccer ball with the best senior varsity players, and suddenly, I couldn't even walk without tripping. Apparently, both my ability to talk and to walk had taken a hit with Emmy's arrival. I walked to the front door of her house, which was also weird to me. I couldn't even remember the last time I knocked at this door. Normally, I entered through the kitchen door, to which I still had a key, or the veranda that opened right into her bedroom that she never remembered to lock because the Emmy I knew rarely worried about anything. Growing up, I don't know how many times I walked into her room with the door unlocked, and half of the time she would be sound asleep. As I raised my hand to knock on the door, her older brother opened it before I could even knock.

"Brad," I greeted him and gave him the pat on the back hug that guys give each other. "You came home."

"Emerson and I came home," Brad corrected me as he walked toward the kitchen. "My parents are still doing a grand tour of surgeries in Europe. You talked to Em today?"

"No, I saw her." I hesitated for a moment. "But we didn't actually get the chance to talk, so I thought I would catch her here." I was not an idiot; Brad was Emmy's older brother. Even though the guy tolerated me as a child, I knew he would always have Emmy's best interest at heart. I was more concerned about getting across to him that I had the same.

Brad nodded at me slowly. "She's not home yet."

"Seriously, school ended over a half hour ago?" It had never occurred to me that she wouldn't be behind the door when I knocked.

"She had somewhere to go."

"The cemetery?" I asked as I tried to piece the puzzle together. "Maybe I should drive there, so she doesn't have to be alone."

"Matt, no." Brad gestured for me to sit. "Emerson's been back for less than twenty-four hours since our esteemed parents shoved her out of here on a plane. There are things she's been through that you and I won't ever fully understand. He was my little brother too, but the connection between Pete and Em was different. She sat in his room for three hours last night just looking around at his things. She didn't talk. She didn't even cry. She just sat there and touched his stuff."

"I loved Pete, too." And that was true. I did love their younger brother as if he were my own. I'd spent so much time with Emmy that I was bound to be around Pete a lot; he would merrily follow us everywhere. He was the happiest damn kid I had ever met. He never threw a tantrum. He didn't require being leashed to Emmy or me when we took him somewhere with us. Right before he got sick, I had started to teach him how to play soccer. For hours, he would scramble all over the field trying to imitate what I did. At our last soccer lesson, he dressed just like me and asked to be called "Matty the Second" all day. Emmy had laughed nonstop from the side where she took pictures; occasionally, she would chase down a ball for us or play because I needed another person to teach him something. For the most part though, she was happy to just sit and watch. Some days, it was still hard even for me to reconcile those moments with his last ones. He looked so sick and so tiny in the hospital with tubes going every which way and the morphine drip that slowly eased him out of the pain and out of the world. Even then, he spent his last times awake holding Emmy's hand and telling her it would be okay without him. He tried so hard not to cry for his sister's sake, and Emmy clutched at him as though her embrace could keep him alive for longer. In the fourteen years I had known her, it was the one and only time I ever saw Em look desperate. Emmy was still holding his hand when the heart monitor flat lined; she didn't let go for a long time. "I was in the hospital room too the night he passed away."

"I know."

I knew Brad knew; he was the only other person in the room. Their parents couldn't watch their son die knowing that medicine had failed him. They failed him. Both of the Caulfields were world-renowned surgeons with more degrees from Ivy Leagues than I could remember, but apparently, cancer doesn't care if your parent is a surgeon or not because cancer hit Pete with a vengeance. After the first or second day, they stopped visiting Pete in his room and took on more work. Pete asked for them once or twice. When they never came, he quit asking for them. Emmy never left his bedside except for the one time he made her so he could talk to me. Even then, she stood feet outside of the door. Brad rarely left either. I only left to go to school. At the end, we were the three he wanted in the room when he died. We were the last of his friends and family.

Brad stared off into space for a while before he finally spoke again. "If you love her too, you'll give her time." Staring straight at me, he reiterated, "It's not going to be easy for her."

I nodded and grabbed the keys off the counter. I moved my car over one driveway and slumped against the steering wheel. I was stuck between two brothers' wishes. That conversation that I had with Pete alone, he'd made me promise him something. Before he even asked, I'd agreed. To be honest, I thought he was going to ask me to take care of his fish or something. At age fourteen, I wasn't really prepared for him to ask me to take care of Emmy and never let her feel alone. Obviously, I hadn't been doing such a good job with that. And now, Brad had asked me to do just the opposite. Normally, I would have asked Emmy what to do, but I guessed I was alone too now.

Emerson

Gratefully, I planned my return to school on a Friday, so I wasn't completely thrown into the three-ringed circus. When I finally summoned the strength to drag myself away from Peter's gave, I walked home spent. I knew it would be hard. Every day had been difficult since Peter died. Sometimes I'd get so mad at him for leaving me by myself. Dying is easy; living is the crappy part. And then I'd hate myself for thinking that way. Peter didn't want to leave. His life was shoved out of his body without his permission or control just like life remained in mine even on days when I wanted to quit. And there were plenty of days in the last two years that I willed life to leave me the way it had left Peter. I learned the hard way that life doesn't exactly take special requests.

When I walked in the door, I could smell the Chinese food takeout coming from the kitchen. Given that neither Brad nor I liked to cook, I wasn't surprised by the smell. I walked toward the kitchen where my brother was taking containers out of a bag and setting up two place settings.

"I figured if I put the take out on plates, we would almost be civilized adults," my brother remarked looking up at me.

"Good call," I said as I started to inspect the containers. "So I'm civilized and you're the adult?"

"Funny," Brad replied. "Did I get enough of the stuff you like?"

"Yes," I said as I dug a fork into a container ignoring the plate after all. "I haven't eaten dinner with someone in two years. My dinner conversation skills might be lacking."

"Our parents didn't have hired help in the house in Paris?" Brad asked as he jerked his head up to look at me.

"Of course, they did. The help just wasn't allowed to eat with me or do anything that would make them more than a server.

When have our parents ever been kind to the people who work for them? They had their own quarters."

"I'm sorry. I should have gotten you out sooner."

"You got me out as soon as you could," I replied honestly.

"Matt came after school to see if you were around." Brad hesitated and looked up. "I wasn't sure if you wanted to talk to him."

"Not particularly," I sighed as I forcefully dug the fork through my noodles. "He'll ask questions, and I won't want to give answers." Two years of silence, and I had come to respect privacy.

"He's your best friend, Em." Brad stared at me intently.

"He was my best friend. Was." To be honest, Matty knew too much and too little at the exact same time. He knew about Peter and all of the tears I'd cried; even as a 14-year-old, he'd stood next to me as my brother died. Matty knew that version of me inside and out, but he didn't know anything about the last two years. Judging by the way he behaved today, our lives had taken two very different trajectories, and I didn't know him anymore than he knew me. "He couldn't even say 'hello' to me when he saw me at school today. His girlfriend, a Hayward, had no trouble yapping at me like she was a Chihuahua, though."

"He's dating a Hayward? How did they make all of their money again?"

"Prostitution," I replied without a single clue. I knew of the Haywards, but I had never interacted with them before. All I knew is that they lived as if they were starring in *Gone with the Wind* or something. Sometimes I wondered if they realized the South lost that war. We live just outside of Raleigh. To be fair, I didn't think that constituted as the Deep South anyway.

"Dealing drugs."

"Bootlegging."

"Cattle-rustling," Brad replied with a straight face.

At that, I started to laugh. Brad did too. For one very short moment, it was nice to laugh with my brother, but then I remembered my other brother who should be sitting here too injecting his crazy ideas. "People change. Circumstances change. Matty was a huge part of my life then, but we can't go back to then."

"No, but you could walk forward."

Sometimes, my older brother annoyed the shit out of me. For now, I was content to stand on my own.

Matt

As I drove up to Savannah's house, I had no idea what the hell I was doing there. As expected, I'd run about seven miles earlier to make up for my missed practice, and the entire time, I could not stop thinking about her. Emerson. She was like a damn Rubik's cube that some idiot scrambled into a haphazard pattern and then just left without fixing. Ironically, the only person I knew who could complete a Rubik's cube, and I mean any Rubik's cube, was Emmy. When we were younger, they tested our IQ in middle school. I was fairly certain Emmy was a genius. Her parents had to be called into the school to have a special meeting with all the principals and her teachers. When I'd asked her if she was the next Einstein, she'd laughed and told me the only thing she had in common with Einstein is her hair looked like his hair when she first woke up in the morning. The thing with Rubik's cubes, sometimes you make them worse when you try to fix them. I didn't want to make her worse, and I also didn't know how to make her better.

"Hey man," Luke peeked into the window of my jeep. "You ready?"

"Yeah, sure," I replied. Luke and I walked around to the back of Savannah house, and I punched in the code to let us into the back gate. The Haywards didn't shy away from flaunting their money in the slightest. They had gargoyles on the front entrance to their house. Gargoyles. As soon as we turned the corner, we could hear the girls giggling in the hot tub.

In bikinis that, as promised, left very little to the imagination, they both jumped up when we arrived.

"Ditch the clothes and come on in," Savannah said with a wink, which sent both of them into hysterical giggles. It looked as though they had already started drinking.

Both Luke and I scrapped our clothes in the guesthouse,

which looked as if it has been set up as some bad honeymoon suite at a cheap motel. Rose petals in the shape of a heart on the bed and a lipstick kiss on the mirror? Seriously?

"Dude, it looks like you're getting laid tonight," Luke said as he gestured to the room.

"I feel like I'm in one of those dumb romance movies the girls always watch," I replied. "Think I'll get money on the bed if I do a real good job?" I batted my eyes at Luke mirroring what I had seen my older sister do hundreds of times.

"She is a Hayward," Luke replied drawing out the name as if he was the rich guy on Gilligan's Island. "And you're too good at batting your eyes. It's kind of freaking me out."

"Not happening tonight." I balled up my clothes and took them outside with my shoes and car keys, so I would have no reason to come back into this room. Luke did the same and followed me back out.

By the time we climbed into the hot tub, Savannah and Eliza were bombed. Weren't you supposed to not drink heavily in those goddamn things? Even though Savannah's hot tub was the size of a small pool, I still felt as if I was trapped in a tiny car when I got into it. At 6 feet 3 inches, it wasn't really that comfortable.

"You could have left your clothes in the guest house." Savannah hiccupped as she scooted her way over to me.

"I figured it would be easier to change to go home later this way," I replied and pushed a piece of hair behind her ears. She took this as an indicator to straddle me. I glanced over, and Luke was already making out with Eliza. Unhelpful bastard.

"Why would you go home tonight when you could stay here with me?" Savannah whispered into my ear and then leaned in to kiss me. The smell and taste of vodka assaulted me. I kissed her back gently as she grabbed roughly at my hair.

"Easy there, Van," I said, unwrapping her arms that were tied around my neck. Christ, this girl was on me like an anaconda.

"You've never complained before," she replied, quickly transitioning from a sloppy drunk to an angry one.

For a moment, I just sat back and looked at her. For the past eight months, I had been dating Savannah Hayward, and I suddenly had no idea why. I didn't care about money; her public shows of wealth embarrassed me. Any idiot would recognize that she was beautiful. At 5 feet 2 inches, she was petite and cute. And when I first met her, she used to smile and laugh all of the time. Now, it seemed fake when she laughed; I felt as if I constantly had a front row seat to the show she was putting on for an audience. Admittedly, I loved having my own personal cheerleader, but was knowing someone would be screaming my name at soccer games worth it? Was I that desperate? "Savannah, I don't think I can do this anymore."

"Do what?" Savannah asked loudly.

"Us. You and me," I replied softly. "It's over." Glancing past Savannah, I saw Luke and Eliza had stopped making out to watch what was unfolding.

"You can't just end us! I'm in this relationship too, and I say when it is done!" Savannah was actually screaming loudly now. "You have no idea what you're talking about right now. Where would you be without me?"

"I guess I am about to find out, right?" I stood up and started to climb out of the hot tub.

She latched onto my arm unexpectedly. "Are you dumping me because of that dumb girl at lunch? She is a nobody. Don't do this!"

"No, things haven't been right between us for a while now." I yanked my hand away from her angrily and stepped out of her reach. "I thought it would get better, but it's just not." I noticed Luke had already climbed out of the hot tub as well. Quickly, I tugged on my shirt and shoes as I left her backyard with Luke quietly following me as Savannah continued to throw a tantrum in the hot tub.

When we reached our cars, Luke stopped me and asked quietly, "This break-up has everything to do with the girl at lunch, huh?"

"I don't know," I replied. "I guess so. Emerson looks like she needs friends now, and Savannah would have never been okay with that."

"You made the right decision," Luke replied. "I figured this was coming soon. I'm on your side, bro." He gave me a quick fist bump and walked to his car.

I put my dry shorts on and climbed into my jeep. Instead of going straight home, I made one quick stop. Despite the sky getting darker, I drove a route that I knew like the back of my hand. For a year straight, I had walked there every single day.

I leaned down and touched the fisherman's hat that had been place on the tombstone. I stared at the engravings for a while before I spoke. "Pete, buddy, I'm going with you on this one. Help me out here. I'm going to need it." I finally knew which brother's request I was going to fulfill.

Emerson

As always, the weekend passed quickly. I guess some things don't really change after all. Instead of going to parties or spending time with friends, I spent the weekend with both of my brothers. I visited Peter's grave every day for at least an hour. On Sunday, Brad went with me, which was nice but also weird. I didn't feel comfortable talking to Peter out loud with someone there.

Last week, by the time I was done talking to the counselors and doing my physical with the school's trainer, I'd only ended up going to two classes. This week, I had to go to all of them. The idea of sitting through eight hours of school did not make me want to get out of bed. I'd always been a good student, but that in itself was the problem. I didn't have to put in all that much effort to get good grades, so I just went through the motions with school. When I was younger, my teachers always wanted to push me ahead a grade or into accelerated classes, but I hadn't wanted it. At the time, I hadn't want to be separated from Matty or my other friends or labeled "special." Prior to Peter's death, I had really enjoyed my nice comfortable bubble. Like all bubbles, mine popped. I didn't feel comfortable in my own skin anymore; some days, I literally didn't know who I was or what I wanted. Those days worried me the most. I was not crazy. Really. I knew Peter was dead and not coming back. I understood all of it. The thing was, I think a part of me died with him that day and like Peter, that part of me was never coming back. I disguised it the best I could. I got out of bed, ate, study, and dressed like a typical teenager. Speaking of, I donned a pair of tiny white shorts and a tight blue T-shirt for my second day of school. The population of our school was 52 percent male to 48 percent female. At least if I could keep dressing in tight clothing, I didn't need to worry about over half of the school seeing through the charade.

I drove myself to school on the second day; my brother has a tough rotation for the next two weeks, so I knew he wouldn't be around too much. As I pulled into the parking lot in my Mini Coop – technically, the car belonged to my parents, which really only fueled my motivation to drive it to a place where it could be easily banged up – I watched all of the other teenagers chatter with friends. Some moved quickly as to not be noticed or bullied while other talked with fake enthusiasm to try to garner the attention of the people around them. At one point in my life, I would have loved being in these dynamics. Right now, I didn't give a damn, so I just grabbed my bag and walked to first period. I felt some eyes glued to me as I walked in the door, and a boy I had never seen before in my life ran to get the door for me. I glanced at him with a frown. Wasted effort, buddy.

Remembering the school from Brad's days here, I easily navigated my way to my first period class and homeroom, AP English Language and Composition. Guidance told me the class only had 12 people including me, so it should be an easy way to start the day. A few people were already there and seated when I walked into the room. As I went to hand my schedule to the teacher, I could hear a few of the other students attempt a British accent.

"Hello, Mrs. Ferguson, my name is Emerson Caulfield. I just transferred back into the district. Guidance told me to give you this note," I amicably handed over the note.

"Are you Brad's little sister?" she asked as she scanned the note.

"Yes. He's in residency now," I filled in for her.

"Honey, tell him that is terrific and I send my best wishes. And well, the last time I saw you, you were in pigtails running through the halls. Welcome back, Emerson. You can really sit anywhere you want."

"Thanks, Mrs. Ferguson. I'll try not to run down the halls this time." If she knew Brad and me, she knew about Peter. I'd have to work extra hard to keep up the charade in her class. I took a seat a row back near the door; I liked having the exit in sight. Also, I didn't want to play with the British accent kids; no one should have that much energy in the morning. I also firmly believed that speaking in a British accent didn't make you anything like the Bard anyway. As the class filtered in, I didn't see anyone from my past and sighed in relief. A girl sat behind me, but no one sat directly next to me.

As Mrs. Ferguson started to do roll and announcements came on, I turned to the girl behind me to make sure it wasn't her seat I took.

"Hey, if I took your seat, just let me know. I can move."

"You're fine. No big deal. It's been awhile, but we had a class or two together in middle school. I'm Lexie," she replied, offering a smile that didn't hold any pity in it.

Grateful, I replied, "Emerson. Thanks for letting me keep the seat." As I turned back around, I noticed our class of 13 was becoming a class of 14. Matty entered the room and went straight to Mrs. Ferguson with a note that looked much like mine. Matty was in this class? Unless he had completely changed, the last book Matty actually read for school was one that still had pictures in it. Mrs. Ferguson nodded at him helpfully and directed him to take a seat.

"Em," he said with a nod as he slid into the open desk next to me. "What's up?"

I wanted to ask what he was doing in the class, but Mrs. Ferguson began the class promptly. Apparently, I had lucked out because they were starting a new unit today. And then she pulled out the book. *Catcher in the Rye*. Not so lucky. I didn't want to read a book where a teenager has a mental breakdown because his little brother dies of cancer. Way too close to home. It practically was my home. And she wanted to juxtapose it to *My Sister's Keeper* another book about a sibling with cancer. Couldn't the characters just die the old-fashioned way? Poison and a dagger!

As she passed out books, she spoke about them excitedly and

gave plot synopsis explaining where we were going with each novel. Right after she gave us our reading assignment, she explained, "One of the essential questions of *My Sister's Keeper* is how far are you willing to go to save a sibling's life? Is there a limit?" I looked at Mrs. Ferguson wondering if that was a serious question because the answer was absolutely not. When I first found out my brother had leukemia, I had offered to give my brother all of the blood and bone marrow he needed even if it killed me in the process. In fact, I had begged with the doctors and nurses to use my organs, blood, and marrow. I would have given him every cell in my body. When I became hysterical about this being a reasonable solution, the doctor had pulled me into a separate room to explain that my brother was so sick that he wouldn't even survive the operations even if it was legal to do that. That was the day I found out my little brother was going to die.

Matt

Switching into all of Emmy's classes probably wasn't the subtlest move in the world. Before school, I went to guidance and pled my case that I wanted to be challenged by more "rigorous classes." When the guidance counselor didn't buy that line of bullshit, I broke down and explained the situation. He moved around my schedule to get me into her AP English and AP American History class; I was already in AP Chemistry and AP Calculus with her. Basically, Emmy was going to have to see me all day except for independent study and gym. Clearly, she wasn't coming to me, so I was going to her.

As the day wore on, it became increasingly clear that she was not pleased with her new schedule. By our third class together, she looked downright pissed. When she walked into AP Chemistry and saw me sitting front and center in the class, she grimaced before walking over and handing over her note to the chemistry teacher, Mr. Archibald. With his standard red suspenders and bow tie, Mr. Archibald was the teacher who hated wasting even one precious moment of class time. As such, he never spoke about anything that wasn't Chemistry related. Though many of the students despised Mr. Archibald and his strict classroom policies, I liked the old guy. I really loved the man when he directed Emmy toward the stool next to mine.

"Hey, lab buddy," I said with a smile. I had now managed to say hello to her twice, which was more than came out on Friday.

"How many?" she asked as she pulled out a navy blue binder.

"How many what?"

"Classes are we in together?"

"Everything but independent study and gym," I whispered closer to her ear. Without any notice, she whipped her head around to stare straight at me. Her blue eyes zeroed in on me with a striking intensity, and for a moment, she just stared. Just as quickly, she let out a sigh of exasperation and swiveled her stool back to facing Mr. Archibald. It took me longer to stop staring though. So much about her had changed, but somewhere buried deep in there was my best friend, and I wanted her back. I had already waited two years for her to come back. I could easily wait a few more months even if it meant taking two AP classes that sucked and I wasn't quite sure I could pass on my own.

Emerson

After I stopped at the cemetery for my daily visit with Peter, I went to the grocery store to stock our house with food. I loved Brad, but the only thing he knew about food was how to eat it, so it looked like I would be trying my hand at cooking and keeping the pantry stocked. Three hours later, I successfully made chicken quesadillas. Unfortunately, I also never wanted to look at food again. I packed everything away for the next day and wrote a note for my brother to heat one up if he needed something quick to eat.

When I finally took my books out, the sun was just starting to dip into the sky. Not wanting to waste the few warm weathered weeks I had left, I used the door from my bedroom to get to the pool. I put the lights on surrounding the pool and dutifully took *My Sister's Keeper* to my favorite place to read. While Brad loved baseball fields and Peter loved any place he could fish, I loved the pool. Because no one else really used it when I was growing up, I considered the pool and backyard an extension of my room. I grabbed a pillow off the lounge chair and walked over to the diving board. Walking precariously to the tip, I put the pillow down and then stretched out to read.

There are two groups of readers: those who like to read about characters who are in similar situations to themselves and those who like to read to escape through characters who are nothing like them. Even prior to Peter's death, I'd fallen into the latter group. Why read about a character just like me? I'd lived my story. I wanted to escape to a fantasyland where the only monsters are ones who can be slayed. I wanted to escape into historical stories that happened long before I was born. After AP English, Mrs. Ferguson had stopped me and asked if I could handle reading the two books she had just assigned. It would only make me stand out more in class if I didn't read them, but I did ask her for a pass on participation on days where the subject matter hit a little too close to home. As I settled myself into reading the book, I tried desperately to separate myself from the situation in the novel.

"How's the reading going?" a familiar voice called out to me from the other side of the pool. Matty stood there with his hands in his pockets and one of the books tucked under his arm.

"How did you get in here?" I asked, looking around. When I came out, I locked everything up except my bedroom door.

"Still have a key to your back gate," he replied with a slow smile. "I saw you down here reading and figured I'd say hello."

"Throw any wild parties while the house was empty?" I asked, trying to get to a neutral topic.

"You really think I would do that?" he asked with a heart-breakingly sad look on his face.

"No, I don't. Why did you transfer into all of my classes?" I sat up so that my legs straddled each side of the board. I was wearing running shorts and a tank top rather than a swimsuit, and I didn't want to get dumped in the water

"Because I really love English and History?" Matty smirked at me.

"Try again."

"Because once upon a time, you were my best friend, Em, and I can't pretend you don't exist." Running his hands through his thick, brown wavy hair, he sat down in a chair on the other side of the pool. At one point in my life, I would have run to his side if he had looked at all like he was in pain and the tug to go remained despite my best efforts to shut all emotions off.

"You said it yourself. We 'were' best friends. You don't owe me anything now. We're different people." I did my best to keep my voice at a slow even tone.

"You really think it's that easy? Christ, Emmy, you were my best friend for the first fourteen years of my life, and now I'm supposed to treat you like a stranger?"

"Matt, I'm not the same person I was when I left, and you're probably not either. Even if I had stayed, we may not have remained friends. We're not little kids anymore who were best friends out of convenience."

"You don't think I recognize that you're not the same person? Before you left, you were so full of energy and compassion. And lightness. Now, you look like you're in agonizing pain all of the time. For the most part, you keep it hidden well and keep up some bullshit act, but the pain has been in your eyes since the moment I saw you again."

I sucked in a deep breath of air; Matty's ability to read all of my bluffs was one of the many reasons we shouldn't be friends again. "Matt, I'm sorry, but the girl you were best friends with is gone. I'm not that girl anymore, and I can't go back to being her. Too much has happened. Do you think there is a moment in the day that I don't think about Peter? Do you think I am ever going to forget he existed and what his last few weeks were like? I can't pretend he didn't exist, Matt. Love is not like some faucet you can turn off and on anytime you want."

"Neither is friendship, Em." I just sat and stared at him. To be honest, I wasn't expecting him to put up any kind of fight, and I didn't really know what to say. As I tried to process how to respond, he continued, "You may not be the same girl anymore. I don't know, but I'm not leaving you behind, Emmy. Whenever you're ready, you know where to find me." He stood up and grabbed his book to take with him.

"Matt?" I called out unable to stop myself. "I'm sorry."

He turned to face me once more. "Don't be. I loved Pete too, and I'm willing to wait for you to be my friend again."

"If I can't?" I blinked back the tears because I honestly didn't know how to be friends with Matt anymore or anyone else for that matter. And I knew all too well that blind hope isn't always a good thing.

"You will.

Matt

As I left Emmy's house, I considered hugging her, but she looked like a cat that had been in too many street fights and now was terrified of being cornered. I knew she took Peter's death the hardest out of anyone, but I suddenly wondered what happened to her in the immediate years following Pete's death. The girl who once looked so confident and relaxed now looked tired and paralyzed with goddamn fear. If I wasn't seeing it with my own eyes, I would never have believed a person could change so dramatically. In fifth grade, one of the meaner groups of kids in our class ripped into a new girl who dressed differently and didn't have much money. Within five minutes, Em had half of the group crying and the rest running away. I'm pretty sure no one picked on that girl again.

When I walked into my room, I went over to the boxes on the top shelf of my closet. Pulling one down gently, I thumbed through the contents. In basically every childhood memory I had, Emmy was there. I looked at the last picture taken of us. We were on one of those amusement park rides where they take your picture at some horrendously awful moment. When we got off the ride, we had both laughed at the picture. Emmy hated any rides with drops and, as expected, the camera went off just before we dipped into the largest drop. In the picture, Emmy was holding on to the bar so tightly that every muscle in her arms stood out, and she was laughing. I had my arm across her to help hold her back in the seat, and I was laughing too as I watched her. Before we'd left the park that day, I'd gone back and bought one of the pictures of us. I'd never told her I'd done it, but I liked knowing I was protecting Em in the picture. Growing up, soccer and Em were my two biggest accomplishments in life. Glancing down at the girl still reading on the diving board outside my window, I wondered if I would always be watching Em. Em thought she'd failed to protect Pete, but I'd failed to protect her. We had all failed.

Emmy

As I entered the locker room for my last period gym class, I was exhausted. All I wanted was to go to talk to Pete and get some sleep. Being a high school teenage girl is sincerely awful. Movies and television pretty much lie about the whole experience. I am expected to giggle at the right moments, dress like I care what people think of me, squeal when I recognize any member of the female body walking down the hallway, flip my hair when a cute guy stares at me, and sit through dreadful classes where the teachers basically just read the chapter out loud. Thus, my expectations for gym were low. Yesterday, we just had a class where we learned the "rules of softball." Today, we were actually supposed to play it.

As I changed into my gym gear, I could hear Savannah on the other side of the lockers rattling on to one of her friends. "Matty and I totally aren't completely broken up," she assured the group. "He just feels sorry for that weird girl whose awkward little brother died. My sister was in the same grade as him, and she said he was totally a freak. Matty's being nice because his parents forced him to be. He seriously couldn't care less about her."

I literally could feel my heart beating in my chest and hear the blood pounding in my ears. I walked to the other side of the lockers to face Savannah. "Listen, midget, I couldn't care less about what you say about me or what's going on with Matt, but don't you dare talk about my little brother. At all. Ever. He was too good to be talked about by someone as ugly as you." Without giving her time to respond, I jogged out to the baseball field and started to stretch with the girls who had already changed.

Within minutes, the gym teacher, Coach Rudolph, had all the girls out of the locker room and picking teams for softball. Savannah obviously volunteered to be a team captain, and some other crony of hers chose to be the second captain. As they went through their picks, it was clear that they were going to leave me as the last choice. Did they really think that was going to make me feel bad about myself? That tactic might work if I was still eight years old. As expected, when it came down to the last pick, Savannah just uttered, "You can bat first if you take the new girl." With that, I donned a blue jersey in contrast to Savannah who was wearing red with everything magically matched.

Savannah, of course, took the prestigious job of being pitcher for the other team, and I took the third seat in line to bat. Savannah may have been the worst pitcher I'd ever seen in my life. It was a miracle if she could possibly get the ball past the plate, yet the two girls who batted in front of me swung at every terrible pitch and let themselves be struck out. As I put my helmet on and grabbed a bat, I decided to give Savannah an actual reason to hate me. Controlling my temper has really never been one of my finer qualities.

When she pitched the first ball directly at me, I jumped out of the way. Mr. Rudolph walked out to the pitcher's mound to give her some tips, and I waited patiently to bat again. At her second pitch, I swung wildly at it as the girls before me had done. Savannah laughed and called the girls in the outfield to come in closer. Fantastic, they would have a better seat for the show I was about to give everyone. When she threw her third pitch, I hit the ball squarely at Savannah as hard as I could given her wild pitches. She was too busy cracking up with a friend to notice the ball coming for her, and it smacked her squarely in the chest knocking the wind out of her and causing her to double over.

Dutifully, playing my part, I ran to the mound to see if my favorite pitcher was okay.

"You bitch!" Savannah screamed.

"Savannah, language!" Mr. Rudolph yelled as he too ran to the mound.

"I'm so sorry, Savannah. I didn't know you were going to get hit!" I said in my sincerest voice. Okay, so the sincerity was fake, but really, that was of little importance.

"You tried to hit me on purpose! I know you did!"

"Savannah, how could I possibly have aimed to hit that ball at you? I'm sure you didn't mean to throw the ball at me the first time, and I couldn't even touch your second pitch. There's no way I could have hit the ball directly at you."

"Mr. Rudolph, I want her suspended," Savannah commanded.

"Mr. Rudolph, with all due respect, I couldn't have predicted where that ball would go. If Savannah was paying attention, she could have just ducked or put her glove up, right?"

Mr. Rudolph stepped in to take charge of the situation. "Alright, Savannah, get two girls to help you to the nurse to get checked out."

"Are you going to suspend her?" Savannah asked as she dramatically flopped into her friends' arms.

"No. She couldn't have hit you on purpose, and you weren't paying attention. It was an accident," Mr. Rudolph said as he scratched his neck.

"Mr. Rudolph!" Savannah objected.

"Savannah, go to the nurse now. That's an order. Everyone else go change. No more softball this week." As the girls headed to the locker room and Savannah dramatized her injury, Mr. Rudolph pulled me off to the side.

"What did she say to you?"

"What do you mean, sir?" I did my best to look confused.

"Emerson, I coached your brother for four years. I watched you throw balls up in the air and hit them even as an eight-year-old. I just covered for you, so I want to know what she said that caused you to send a line drive at her."

Realizing I was out of luck, I came clean. "She called my younger brother who passed away a freak, sir. She said other stuff about me, but I don't care about that. And honestly, I didn't know I was going to hit her or where I was going to hit her. I'm not that good." I held my breath as I waited for him to lecture and most likely suspend me.

"Well, that would certainly do it," he replied, studying me. "Emerson, I am sorry about your younger brother. Knowing Brad and you, I'm sure he was one of the best kids around."

"Thank you, sir," I replied as my eyes defied me and filled with tears. "Pete was better than Brad and I put together."

"Take a moment and pull yourself together before you head into the locker room to change."

"You're not going to punish me?" I asked.

"Emerson, I think you've been punished enough. No more contact sports in class though. I can't have you and Savannah out to kill each other every day." With that, he collected the few pieces of baseball equipment lying around and left me standing on the pitcher's mound with tears that I just couldn't hold back anymore.

As I turned around and broke down crying, I felt arms come around me. I looked up to see Luke's face near mine.

"Just hide your face in my shirt," he ordered. "Everyone will think I'm making a move on you."

I nodded my head in affirmation and just cried into Luke's shirt for all the things I had lost and the person I had become.

Matt

"What the hell happened?" I asked Luke as we jogged around the track for soccer practice to warm up. "I've heard rumors that Em tried to kill Savannah, and Savannah tried to get Em kicked out of the school."

"Don't be dumb," Luke replied. "Did you really think Savannah was going to take the breakup lying down?"

"She said something to Em?" I asked as I started to piece the puzzles together.

"She called Peter a 'freak,' and Em got pissed and aimed a softball directly at her 'accidentally.'"

"Did she actually make contact?"

"Dude, you've seen Em hit a baseball. It's like the genes are in her blood or something." Luke turned around and jogged backwards. "Didn't her older brother set all kind of school records in baseball?"

"Yeah, they won the State Championship two of the four years Brad was here. I remember going to the games. Savannah really called Pete a 'freak'?"

"Yeah, man, and something to the effect of you hang out with her because you feel bad for her."

I could feel my blood pressure rising. I wished I could take back ever dating Savannah. To be honest, she was a drunken mistake at a party. I didn't expect to date her as long as I did, and now that I knew who was paying the price for it, I felt even worse.

"Matt, there's more," Luke whispered.

"What else could Savannah possibly have said to hurt her? Christ, she already made fun of her dead brother."

"She's going to send out a mass anonymous message tomorrow that Emerson was in a psychiatric ward for two years because she tried to kill herself after Peter died."

"What?" I barked and stopped running completely as I pulled Luke back with me. I suddenly understood the expression "seeing red."

"I don't know much about Emerson's time in Europe, but Em would never try to kill herself. She knows that Peter would never forgive her for that."

"I know she didn't do it, but that's not what matters. It matters what other people are willing to believe and who has the better gossip. And if Savannah does this tomorrow, Emerson will be a social pariah by the time the lunch bell rings."

"Shit!" I screamed. "She can't go through all of this crap right now. She's still dealing with Pete's death for Christ's sake. I watch her stare at different things sometimes, and I know that she's staring because something reminded her of Pete."

"Dude, I'm on your side." Luke slapped me on the back. "I know Emerson didn't try to kill herself. How far are you willing to go to protect her and change the gossip of the day tomorrow?"

"I'll do anything," I replied without hesitation.

"I hope you mean that because you are going to have to step up to the plate for your girl tomorrow."

"Luke, if you know a way out, I'll do anything to protect Em."

Emerson

I sat at Peter's grave for a long time. With my head buried in my hands, I once again cried more tears than I knew I had in me. "I'm sorry," I sobbed helplessly. I knew my brother. He would have been horrified by my behavior in gym. "Peter, I know I screwed up, and I know you're disappointed with me. I got so mad at her for what she said that I didn't think. I was just angry, and I wanted to hurt her as badly as she hurt me. I'm not like you, Peter. I don't forgive or turn the other cheek. How am I supposed to let this go? How am I supposed to let you go? I can't do it, Peter. I'm so sorry, but I can't do it."

As I drove home, I let the tears dry on my face. I wanted to be reminded of my brother, and today, I would have given my life just to hug him again. To be honest, I'm not sure how I made it home. The cemetery was only a few blocks from my house, but I didn't really remember making the turns or any part of the drive. I just remember arriving in my driveway where I shut the car off and rested my head on the steering wheel.

I woke up to a tapping on my car window. Judging by the sky, I had been asleep for at least two hours. When I looked up, I saw Matty and Lucas standing in my driveway. Pulling myself together quickly, I hopped out of the car.

"Tired?" Matty asked.

"Bad day," I replied as I started to walk toward my house. Unfortunately, they both followed me. I had been hoping that they were just on their way next door to Matty's house.

"Emerson, we need to talk," Luke said. I opened the front door and dropped my stuff in the foyer.

"So talk," I quipped pulling out a soda and a bowl of fruit to eat as a snack.

"Em, Savannah's not going to stop," Matty began hesitantly. "I should have seen this coming when I dumped her. I'm sorry."

"Stop what?"

"Doing everything in her power to make your life miserable," Luke said. The two of them kept exchanging what I'm sure they thought were subtle looks.

"Well, someone should really tell her that I'm already miserable, so she should save her energy for something else." I didn't make eye contact with either of them for a second although I had a feeling they both knew what I was about to admit. "We all know I purposely drilled her with a ball today. I shouldn't have done that."

"She shouldn't have brought up Peter," Matt answered quickly, looking as angry as I had ever seen him.

"Kids, in case you are forgetting, we have bigger problems," Luke interrupted giving Matt a sideways glance.

"What? Savannah is going to throw a basketball at my head tomorrow? I'll live. Please just drop it." I wanted nothing more than for this conversation to end. I wasn't at the point with Luke or Matty that I wanted to discuss anything of significance.

"Em, Savannah is going to send out an anonymous message on all social networks tomorrow afternoon that you tried to kill yourself and spent the last two years in a psychiatric ward," Luke finished and looked up at me.

I was shocked. Not that Savannah would do something like that but because it wasn't all a lie. I had thought about killing myself a lot in the past two years; I never told anyone, but in my mind, it was my escape route for when I couldn't take it anymore. I know it would upset Brad and disappoint my parents, but every day was a fight. A fight to breathe. A fight to not cry. A fight to talk to people. Hell, a fight just to get out of bed in the morning. And in less than 24 hours, all of my ugliest and darkest thoughts would be at the forefront of everyone else's mind

"We know that's not what happened, Emmy," Matty said softly and put his arm around me.

I was too numb to push him away. "So that's it? Tomorrow, I

won't be the girl whose brother died. I will be the girl who tried to kill herself." Instinctively, I curled into Matty more. I needed just one second of comfort to face the storm that was brewing.

"We thought of a way out," Matty whispered.

"Em, you have to strike first this time," Luke said forging ahead. "You have to do something before Savannah starts the rumor tomorrow so that the attention is on you for another reason."

"Like what? Flashing the school? Having a public girl fight? No thanks." I crawled out of Matty's arms. "We all make choices, Luke. Today, I decided to try to beam Savannah with a ball. Tomorrow, she is going to spread the rumor. We both made a decision."

"While I wouldn't mind seeing either of those things, it's not what I was thinking." Luke glanced hesitantly at Matt. "You need to start dating Matt."

"What?" My eyes widened in surprise. I took a step farther back from Matt.

"Let Matt's popularity shield you. When the rumor comes out about you trying to commit suicide, no one will believe it if you are dating one of the most popular guys in the grade. And with the way you and Savannah went at it today in gym, people will believe she or one of her zombies is going after you for dating Matt."

"How do you even know this rumor is going to happen?" I asked.

"Eliza told me," Luke replied.

"You're still dating her?" Matt asked seemingly surprised. Maybe he hadn't realized yet that we all have our secrets.

"Behind Savannah's back, yes. Eliza called me the night you broke up with Savannah and said she hoped we could keep going out."

"How do you know she's being honest with you?" I asked, trying to wrap my head around how each player fit into the complex game I had entered. "Eliza is Savannah's best friend. Why would she help me?"

"She told me the honest story of what happened today in the locker room. Seriously, she said that Savannah deserved the ball to the head. I think Eliza would stop being friends with her if she wasn't so afraid of the consequences." Luke rubbed the tension out of his neck as he spoke.

"So essentially she doesn't want to end up like me?" I asked, even though I already knew the answer.

"We can change how this plays out, Em," Matt interjected. "It's time to play offense instead of defense."

"We haven't even really talked at school, Matt. How the hell are we going to convince anyone that we are now the school's favorite couple?" I asked.

"By putting on one hell of a show tomorrow morning," Luke answered.

Matt

As planned, Luke and I arrived at school earlier than normal the next morning. We parked our cars front and center in the student parking lot.

"You are going to have to chill, man," Luke interrupted my thoughts. "I can actually see the wheels turning in you idiotic brain. You need to look like the most relaxed and happiest guy in the world today. Quit brooding."

"Don't be an ass," I snapped back.

"Why don't you focus on that instead?" Luke tilted his head toward the other side of the lot.

Emerson was walking toward us, and she looked stunning. With her sunglasses tangled in her messy bun, she smiled as if she didn't have a care in the world. In her blue and white striped top and yellow shorts, she looked as if she had stepped off a yacht and into the parking lot. I let my eyes roam down her long legs to reach her flats.

"Well, you are doing a hell of a job of looking like you want to maul her." Luke slapped my back. "Good work, man." Unfortunately, I wasn't acting.

I didn't even turn to look at him. As my eyes met Emmy's, all of the anxiety drained out of me. She gave me a smile and a slight nod. When she reached us, I didn't hesitate as I grabbed her to pull her into me. She dropped her bag and hopped up into my arms so that her long leg wrapped around my waist. As if we had done this a thousand times before, I locked my hands under her butt to help support her.

"Hi," she said softly.

"Em," I started, startled by how much my voice croaked. Christ, it was as if I was going through puberty all over again.

She giggled softly at the sound. "Kiss me, Matt. We don't need to talk."

Tilting my head down, I gently pressed my lips to hers. As I felt her hands play with the back of my hair, I pulled her to me tighter and parted her lips with mine. Startled, she moaned slightly in the back of her throat. And that was my undoing. I broke the kiss suddenly and rested my forehead against hers. This time, I managed to speak. "Em, you are, without a doubt, the most beautiful girl I've ever seen."

For a second, she searched my eyes and then she leaned back in to kiss me. This time, she kissed with more urgency, and I matched her kiss for kiss. When she stopped, she smiled gently at me and then unwrapped her legs to slide gracefully to the ground. Neither of us moved away though; we both stayed wrapped in each other's arms and stood still.

"It's about goddamn time," Luke yelled as he clapped and cheered for us.

I knew it was all part of the plan, but the plan went out the proverbial window the second I had seen her this morning. I had a new plan that involved a lot more of kissing her. In my arms, she turned to see the size of the crowd watching us. I looked up for the first time too. It looked like half of the student body was surrounding us. Savannah stood near the side watching us with fire in her eyes.

I grabbed Em's hand and bowed dramatically for the crowd. "We'll be here for as long as she lets me keep kissing her like that," I yelled out to the crowd.

Within an instant, they all started whistling, clapping, and hollering. With her hand hiding her blushing face, Emmy gave a slight bow as well. The crowd ate it up and cheered louder. I wrapped my arms around her from behind her and kissed her still slightly rosy cheek. As I felt her relax into my arms as Luke began chatting with her, I realized that I had loved Em my whole life. I knew I loved her as my best friend, but it suddenly occurred to me that I had always been in love with her. Emmy had always been my everything. Tilting my head upward, I silently thanked Peter for seeing what I had been too dumb to see.

Emerson

"Explain to me again why we are going to watch a soccer game," Brad asked as he pulled into the parking lot next to the soccer field fairly early on a Saturday morning.

"Because I'm fake dating Matty, and a girlfriend would go to her boyfriend's soccer game," I explained for what seemed like the twentieth time.

"And why are you fake dating him?"

"Because his ex-girlfriend started a horrible rumor, and dating Matt basically replaced the rumor." I was absolutely stunned that Luke and Matty's plan worked so well. When the rumor hit about me trying to kill myself, it didn't even matter. Everyone was so into the gossip about me and Matty that they chalked up the rumor to someone being jealous of me. A few people I didn't even know stopped me to tell me how great Matty and I were together and how dumb the rumor was. The last great plan of Luke's I had partaken in was toilet papering a police officer's house and then running like hell when the lights came on inside. So far, this planned worked out a lot better.

"What was the rumor exactly?" Brad asked as he parked the car.

"It's not important now," I replied, getting out of the car. I really did not want to tell my older brother what the rumor was because he'd worry more about me than he already did. He'd also probably want Savannah's head on a stick *Lord of the Flies* style, which actually wasn't all that unpleasant a picture.

"Why am I here?" Brad asked with a yawn. I had dragged him out of bed this morning to come to the game with me. Neither of us were exactly morning people

"Because the two people I trust right now are both soccer players, and I don't like sitting by myself." I answered honestly. Trying to boost his ego, I continued, "Plus, I wouldn't want to deprive people of the chance of seeing how good-looking and successful you have become."

"I was good-looking then. You'd laid it on a little too thick with that last one."

"Well, it's always better to overachieve, right?" I asked, mocking a poster he used to have in his room in high school.

"Just remember our deal." Brad started climbing the bleachers to get a seat.

I followed him like an eager little puppy. "I know. Nap. And then we go for a run after the game." Brad hated running, but he knew I used to love it. This deal was his not so subtle way of trying to push me back into an activity I once did. We sat down about halfway up the bleachers. I watched as Matty and Luke warmed up with the rest of the team. To further cement our relationship, Matty had given me his away game jersey to wear to the game. Nothing like being branded to show you are dating someone.

"Your fake boyfriend is waving to you," whispered Brad.

I looked down at the field again, and I did see Matty waving at me. Laughing at his over the top enthusiasm about it, I waved to him back. Once he was satisfied with my wave, I started to scan the crowds for people I knew. I saw Lexie from my English class sitting with some guy I didn't know. Toward the front, I saw Savannah and Eliza in their cheerleading uniforms trying to rally the crowd. Even though Eliza was prettier and a better cheerleader from what I could tell, Savannah made sure to stay front and center.

"Em, Matty's sister is here, and I think she's going to come sit with us," Brad interrupted my thoughts.

Looking at the crowd walking toward the bleachers, I finally spotted Mallory. She looked like a terrifyingly skinny skeleton draped in skin as she walked toward us. "What happened to her?" I asked in a hushed voice.

"She's anorexic. Don't mention food or weight or how she

looks," Brad whispered as she climbed toward us.

I could not believe this was the same girl I had dressed up as when I was little. As a child, I used to love watching Mallory get ready for dates. She had the thickest and prettiest brown hair I'd ever seen. It had a natural shine and wave to it. Like Matty, she had breathtaking eyes. I always hoped her prettiness would rub off on me as a little girl.

"Hi, Brad, Emmy!" Mallory greeted us in a cheerful voice. "Do you mind if I sit with you for the game?"

"Not at all," Brad replied, easily giving her a quick hug and then stepping back so she could enter row.

"Hi, Mallory. It's good to see you again," I offered. She grabbed me quickly to hug me. I could feel every bone in her back as she hugged me. I held onto her loosely afraid of how fragile she was.

"I'm so glad you and Matt are dating. I've been waiting for you two to get together since you used to make him marry you every day when you were three."

"What? I don't remember that." Confused, I looked between her and Brad.

"You don't remember that?" my older brother asked with a chuckle.

"When the two of you were three, you were obsessed with weddings. You would get all dressed up in white. Sometimes you wore a dress. Sometimes you wore a bed sheet draped around you toga style, and you would make me or Brad officiate the wedding where you two pledged to always share your gummy worms and let each other win sometimes." Mallory smiled at the memory.

"And Matty let me drag him down the aisle every day?" I asked.

"Em, Matt has done whatever you wanted since you were born," Brad interjected. "Hey, I see a few teachers I used to have. I'm going to go talk to them. You two fine by yourselves?"

"Yes, Bradley. Don't let us stop you from soaking up praise." I used his full name because I knew he hated it,

Messing up my hair, he walked down to talk to his teachers. As the game started, I dutifully watched to the best of my ability. Whenever Matty or Luke scored, I jumped up and cheered and yelled as loud as I could. At one point, Matt waved up to the two of us, and I waved back absentmindedly.

"How have you been, Mallory?" I asked turning to my companion.

"Good," Mallory replied, studying her designer shoes. "I moved back home this past year after I finished grad school for teaching. I'm just figuring out where to go from here, you know?" I nodded. In a way, I knew exactly what she meant. I'd spent the last two and a half years trying to figure out where to go from here.

"Do you want to teach?" I asked carefully.

"I don't know." Mallory turned to look at me. "My freshman year of college, I fell in love with a guy two years older than me."

"Cole?"

"Yeah, I really loved him. He was going to be a doctor, and we got engaged the day I graduated. I'm not sure I ever really planned on working. I just wanted to be his wife and have children. Then one day, he abruptly ended it and called off the engagement. I found out later that he was sleeping with someone in his med school class."

"I'm so sorry, Mal." I grabbed her hand and squeezed it lightly.

"I was dumb. I should have known I wasn't good enough for him." Mallory studied her shoes again.

"It sounds like it was the other way around. He didn't deserve you." Just as I thought I was making headway with Mallory, I noticed Savannah snaking up the bleachers toward us. Without hesitating, I stretched out my long legs to the row in front of us and leaned back. I wanted Savannah nowhere near me.

"Hey, Mallory, Emerson," Savannah called out in a cheerful

voice as she approached us.

"Hi, Savannah," Mallory dutifully greeted her.

"It's good to see you, Mallory! Wow, it looks like you've put on a bunch of weight since that last time I saw you! You should still count your calories though so you don't put on too much," Savannah suggested in a helpful tone though she looked like the cat who had just swallowed the canary.

Mallory paled and withered next to me. "Savannah, as always it is a pleasure," I started. "While we're talking about looks and stuff, girl to girl, you'd probably get more guys if you didn't look like a prepubescent twelve-year-old. I guess there's always implants, but most guys seem to like the real thing." Sometimes, I had no idea where the venom that I spewed came from. I had all this hatred boiling inside of me that just seemed to explode at the slightest provocation.

"Emerson, I hope your next attempt at suicide sticks," Savannah whispered cruelly though I could tell by her face that I got the better of her this time. With a quick pivot and a stomp, she stomped down the stairs.

I turned to look at Mallory who was still pale as a ghost and visibly shaking. "Mal, she only said that stuff to you because she's pissed at Matt and me. Forget about her. She has the IQ of a low-watt light bulb."

After a few shaky breaths, Mallory stood up. "I should go. I'm not feeling well all of the sudden."

"Brad and I can take you home," I offered quickly, afraid she would pass out walking by herself.

"No, it means a lot to Matt that you are here. You are going to be the first person he wants to hug after the game. Tell him he played great and I'll see him at home." Without looking back, she walked tentatively down the bleacher steps just as Brad was headed back up to me.

"Where is she going?" he asked, handing me a drink.

"Home. Matt's ex appeared and told Mallory that she looked

like she was gaining weight, and she should keep counting her calories." I took a sip of my Coke.

"Well, shit," Brad replied, looking out at the crowd, but Mallory had already disappeared.

With thirty seconds left on the clock, the two teams were tied. Both Brad and I cheered for Matt who had control of the ball. Making it look effortless, Matty dribbled the ball past two defensive players for the opposing team and took a clean shot at the goal. It went in just as the game buzzer sounded.

"Go congratulate your fake boyfriend," Brad said as he clapped. "I'll meet you at the car."

Making my way down to the field, I had no idea how I would find Matty. Apparently, everyone flooded the field after a win. Just as I was about to give up, he appeared in front of me.

"Good game, boyfriend," I said helpfully. "That last shot was amazing." Without any warning, he pulled me up into his arms so that we were face to face. He kissed me with the same urgency I felt in all of his kisses. Giving in, I wrapped my arms around him and sucked on his bottom lip gently. As far as fake boyfriend's go, he wasn't the world's worst kisser.

When he finally dropped me, he held onto my hands. "Thanks for coming, Em. It means a lot to me."

I quickly leaned forward and kissed his cheek while I squeezed his hands. "Brad's waiting for me by the car, so I'll see you tonight, okay?" Without waiting for an answer, I kissed him again on the lips and then pulled away to head to the car.

Matt

Emerson and I had been "dating" for the last two weeks. We held hands and kissed in public places at school. After about the third day, she quit tensing up every time I put my arm around her or touched her, which I considered a step forward. We had done such a good job that we had everyone convinced we were in fact a legitimate couple. To be honest, I was becoming increasingly convinced that we were dating, which was becoming a problem because I wanted to take her on actual dates. Convincing her to go to my soccer game had been a hard fought victory. When I'd asked if she wanted to go to a soccer team party, she'd looked at me as though I were crazy. She finally broke down when I told her we could leave whenever she wanted.

As I walked to the door to pick her up, I felt jittery. Christ, I was turning into a 13-year-old girl. I wanted her first party to go smoothly. I wanted to convince her that I could take care of her. I also really wanted to make out with her. I knocked on her door and waited patiently.

"You knocked?" Emmy asked as she swung open the door.

"Well yeah, I thought you might be creeped out if I used my keys." I fumbled through the words.

"Hasn't stopped you before," Emmy noted as she stepped back so I could enter the house. She looked in the mirror in the foyer as she snapped in her diamond studs.

"I don't ever really want to be on the wrong side of you and a baseball bat," I pointed out for her.

Frowning, she turned to me. "Do I look like I should be going to a high school party?"

As she pivoted for me and I took in her jeans and sleeveless black turtleneck that was completely open in the back, I let out a whistle. Her hair was piled neatly on top of her head to show off her back. "You look amazing."

She smiled as she glance at me in my dark-blue Oxford shirt and khaki cargo shorts. "Not too bad," she commented.

"The party is just two roads over. I didn't know if you wanted to walk or me to drive."

"Let's walk," she replied grabbing her keys and cell phone.

"Are you sure?" I asked glancing down at her very spiky heels.

"I'm fine in these, and I should keep my legs stretched out after Brad's run of tears today."

"You're running again?" A long time ago, Emmy used to love to run, and she was damn good at her. Her long legs gave her a graceful run and the ability to jump hurdles without much difficulty.

"I wouldn't necessarily call what I did today running. Do you remember the way I used to run as a kid with my arms stretched out because I thought I could fly if I went fast enough? Well, that looked about three times better than whatever it was I was doing today."

"You want to go with me on my run tomorrow?" I asked. I don't know how Brad got her out running again, but I'd run on my off day if it meant that Emmy started doing something again. Unlike Em, I hated running. In soccer, running was just a means to the goal for me.

"I saw you run today. I'll pass. You're in better shape than Brad, and I could barely keep up with him."

"Oh, come on. I'll let you set the pace. We can go for an elderly person speed walk if you want," I baited her. Challenging Emerson was always the most likely way to get her to do something. She would never admit it, but she absolutely hated to lose at anything. When we were little, sometimes she would hold silent competitions in her head and then randomly just announce that she'd won. I mean, she was gracious about losing and everything, but normally, she had a wait time of five minutes before wanting to try again in order to win.

"Fine," she sighed with exasperation, "but I get to sleep in before we go."

"No problem. We're here." I gestured up at the somewhat crowded house standing before us. "Are you ready?"

"I get asked that question a lot lately. Let's go." Em reached down and grabbed my hand. I gave her hand a quick squeeze to let her know that I was nearby.

When we entered the party, it was in full swing. Most people held cups. Some were dancing while others were just standing around talking. The house belonged to a senior on the soccer teams whose parents frequently went out of town; I had been enjoying the benefits of his lack of adult supervision since freshmen year. As I walked Emmy to the kitchen island where all the drinks were set up, I suddenly had no idea if she had been to a high school party before or if she even drank.

I leaned down to whisper to her. "If you don't want to drink, I don't have to."

"Shot of vodka," she replied as she took in the various types of alcohols.

As I poured the two shots, I watched her eyes scan the party. I wondered if she was looking for Savannah. When I got home from soccer, Mallory had been holed up in a bathroom crying because of Savannah's remarks. If Savannah had a clue what was good for her, she would stay far away from this party. As I also scanned the party, I became increasingly aware of all the guys who were eying up Emmy. Placing my hand on her lower back, I instinctively pulled her closer.

"Isn't Luke dating Eliza?" Em asked suddenly as she stared at Luke and some blonde who I thought was named April. I could never remember people's names when they were named after months.

"Luke doesn't really date one person consistently. He dates around a lot and has no intention of getting serious with any of them."

"But Eliza's here." Em jerked her head to the side. "Is he really going to make out with some other girl in front of her?"

"Most likely." I didn't really understand why Em cared unless she had a thing for Luke.

"How is this okay? How are you okay with this?" She slammed back her shot quickly and helped herself to another refill.

Not waiting for my answer, she marched over to where Luke was blatantly flirting on the back porch. I followed on her heels. To be honest, I was more concerned with another guy hitting on her or her having a thing for my best friend than I was at her yelling at Luke. Better him than me.

Depositing herself between the blonde and Luke, Em leaned onto his shoulder and with a tipsy slur said, "Excuse me," to the blonde who looked very put out. "This isss going to be aaaaawhile." Looking highly annoyed, the blonde hightailed it out of there.

"Is she drunk?" Luke asked me.

"She had two shots," I responded. Maybe that was enough to put her under.

Without warning, she smacked Luke on the back of the head. "What the hell are you doing, Luke?" She had certainly sobered up fast.

"What are you talking about?" He went to grab her wrists, but I pinned her to me instead.

"You know Eliza likes you. Like actually likes you. She's here, and you're flirting with some dumb blonde trying to rack up soccer players."

"You do realize the irony of you calling someone a dumb blonde?" Luke asked as he gestured to her hair.

"Ass, I've been here like two weeks, and I already know that June's main goal is to sleep with the entire soccer team," she replied. Inwardly, I was proud of myself. I knew the girl had a month for a name. That should count for something.

"I don't date, Emerson. Relationships are fleeting. You are normally the first one to point that out lately." I was really hoping he was wrong about that if I ever got Em to admit that we were an actual couple, which was already an uphill battle.

"Your little brother didn't die," Emerson fired back. Apparently, she wasn't drunk in the slightest.

"Your mom didn't walk out on you, your dad, and your little sister," Luke replied, taking a long swig from his beer bottle. Luke's mom had abruptly walked out on them about a year ago. I don't think they have heard from her since. Outwardly, his little sister took it the hardest, but Luke's status of a player began around the time his mother left them.

"I'm sorry about your mom, Luke. My parents walked out of the job of being parents a long time ago," she said softly.

"Then, you should understand. Why care about people who are only going to leave? It's easier this way."

"For you, maybe. Not for Eliza. And I came back."

"Yes, Emerson, your body came back. I'm not sure where the rest of you went though." He glared at her.

"Luke, shut the hell up, man." I used my free arm to shove him.

"It's fine," Emerson grabbed my arm. "You don't have to like me. Eliza, though, she's not a bitch. She told you the truth about Savannah. She came to this party without Savannah, which I'm sure she did for you. And you don't think this girl is worth more than hooking up with once? She's terrified of Savannah, but she's doing all of this stuff for you, Luke."

At that moment, Eliza appeared at the porch door.

"Eliza," Emerson greeted her with a smile. "I know it's best for me to stay away from you, but I wanted to say thank you."

"It was the right thing to do. Savannah's been my best friend since I can remember, but she's crossing lines with stuff she's doing and saying. I can't really go against her publicly because she knows every single secret I have."

"If you do have to stand up to her eventually, we'll have your back, Eliza," I confirmed. When I looked down at Emmy to see if she was in agreement, she was beaming at me.

"We all have secrets," Emerson told her, sharing a pointed look with Luke.

"You want a drink, Eliza?" Luke asked as he put out his arm. "I'm empty."

Looking grateful, Eliza gave a quick smile to Em and me and then settled into Luke's arm as they walked back into the house.

When we were alone, I looked down at Emerson who was staring at me. "What?" I quickly ran my hand over my face to make sure I didn't have anything on it.

"Thank you." She kissed me quickly on the cheek. I pulled her in closer to me as I rubbed her bare back. "Let's make a bet. Whichever one us can single handedly win a three cup game of flip cup gets to make the other person do something of his/her choice."

"You sure about that?" I asked.

"Yep, let's go." She grabbed my arm and pulled me into the family room where they were having flip cup tournaments. Looking around the room, it looked as though a lot of seniors were really honing their flip cup abilities for college. Their parents would be so proud. Em let go of my hand to whisper something into our host's ear.

"Well, we have a challenge ladies and gentleman," Tyler yelled as he clapped his hands together. All activity in the room ceased. "Our lovely Emerson has challenged our fine Matthew to a two person flip cup tournament of three cups of the finest beer." The "finest" was surely some cheap beer that would taste like toilet water. It wasn't my first round of flip cup at Tyler's house. "Do we have anyone who wants to make a wager?"

"I have fifty dollars on Matty," Luke screamed from the corner. Eliza was cuddled into his lap. "I'm betting Princess Emerson has never flipped a cup in her life considering all the fine china that surrounds her." Sometimes, I really wanted to kick Luke's ass. He was being an ass and he knew it.

"I'll put fifty dollars on Emerson," Tyler replied as another soccer player set up three cups on each side of the table, each half filled with beer.

Emmy now stood across the table from me. She leaned in with a laugh and said, "May the best neighbor win." I shook my head at her. I had been playing flip cup for years now; she was in for a rude awakening. I wanted to win the bet. There were certainly some things I could think of that I wanted.

We both kept our hands behind our back until Tyler shouted, "Go!"

Without a second thought, I chugged down my first beer in one long gulp. Emmy was still drinking as I set the cup down to flip. It took me three tries to flip it and by that time, Emmy had caught up and flipped her cup. Reaching for my second beer, I also chugged it down quickly. When I looked across, Emmy was getting ready to flip her second cup too. Shit. I moved faster. It only took me two tries to flip mine. As Emmy and I both reached for our final beers, I couldn't chug with the same ease as I had done the first two. I finished my final beer, just as she flipped her last cup. The room broke into thunderous applause for her. She laughed and held up one of her empty cups. Moving around the table, she jumped into my arms still laughing.

"We have a winner! Pay up, Luke!" Tyler announced. Luke begrudgingly handed Tyler his money. Without anyone but me seeing, Tyler slipped Emmy some of his winnings.

"You played me," I replied, astonished.

"Only a little." She held up her hand to indicate only the tiniest amount.

"Well, what do you want?" I asked. I really hoped that she wanted what I would have wanted which would be some privacy to make out.

"A piggyback ride home," she replied. "My legs are killing me."

"Alright, I get one dance, and then we'll go." I scooped her up and carried her to where people were dancing in the living room. As we entered, a slow song started to play. Pulling her close, I wrapped my arms around her lower back while she wrapped her arms around my neck. She rested her head on my shoulder as we swayed gently. As we danced, I thought of all the times I had danced with Emmy. Chicken dances when we were little. Her tenth birthday when she desperately wanted to be a salsa dancer and I was her ungraceful partner. Our eighth grade dance at Halloween. Shifting so she would have to look at me, I leaned down and kissed her when our eyes met. She stood on her tiptoes so her lips would reach mine with little problem. I let my two hands roam over back, and she grabbed my shirt to pull me in tighter. It was the best kiss of my life.

Emerson

After our kiss, Matty piggybacked me home as promised. The slight problem was that he was a good deal more wasted than me. We zig-zagged a lot on the walk home. I thought about inviting him in, but I didn't know where that would go. He was a bit drunk and a lot flirtatious that night, and there was too much history between us to talk about anything when he was drunk. I didn't really know that I wanted to tell him the full story when he was sober either, but it seemed I was glued to Matty for the time being. I had no real interest in dating anyway, and he understood it was a charade. At least, I thought, he remembered that it was a charade. Sometimes when he looked at me, I wondered if he was just the world's greatest untapped actor or he genuinely believed we were dating. I really preferred the first option.

Not tired yet, I pulled a box of pictures out from under my bed. The first one was of Brad, Pete, and me with our faces all squished together making weird faces. The picture had been taken when Peter was in the hospital. Peter had been used to me having a camera glued to my hand, and he'd told me he didn't want me to stop taking pictures just because he was dying. I'd taken the picture, and it had broken my heart. We had taken a lot of pictures that day. I'd put Peter's favorite in his casket when we buried him. Most days, I wished I had put myself in there. Luke was right about me. I was physically there, but emotionally, I was six feet under with my little brother and had been since the day he died. It really should have been me. Other than leukemia, Peter was able to bounce back from anything. If he fell, he got up. If someone said something that hurt his feelings, he brushed it off without second thought. If he embarrassed himself, he was the first to laugh. As I wiped the renegade tear from my eye, I touched his picture as if it would bring me closer to him. After all, I had come back to feel closer to him, and so far, all I felt I was doing was failing miserably.

Before I closed the box and the memories that I didn't know if I should embrace or hide from, one last picture fell out at me. It was of Matty and me on some terrifying rollercoaster that I had let him coerce me into going on despite the fact that at the time I was severely afraid of heights and falling. As if the rollercoaster itself was not bad enough, the ride had one of those cameras where it took a picture of you at the worst possible moment. To be fair, any moment that I was on a rollercoaster was a bad enough moment for me. It was one of the last pictures taken of me before Peter was diagnosed with leukemia. As I studied the picture closely, I realized how happy I looked despite my fear. I couldn't stop screaming and laughing, and Matty had put his arm across me to keep me safely tucked against the back of the ride. I went back to get the picture because I had a crush on Matty back then. He was my best friend, and he made me laugh. And despite the fact that girls were already whispering about how cute he was, I was always his first choice when it came time to picking partners or picking teams. In middle school, that meant just about everything, but middle school was over now. That part of my life was over now. It was impossible for me to just return to being that carefree girl who trusted in everything and everyone.

I ripped the picture into small little pieces. It was pointless to wonder "what if" in regards to my relationship with Matty. "What if" was destroyed by "what actually happened" a long time ago.

Matt

As Em and I grabbed a table at lunch on Monday, I watched Luke amble over to us. I hadn't spoken to him since he and Emmy went at it at Tyler's party, so I had no kind of idea what mood he was in today.

"Hey," he said as he dropped his lunch onto the table and scooted into the bench across from us.

"I shouldn't have yelled at you at the party," Emmy blurted out quickly. I was a bit astonished; apologies from Emmy were hard to come by these days.

"Don't worry about it," he said with a shake of his head. "For what it's worth, I am really sorry. I came back and assumed everyone else's lives had gone on without a hitch, and I shouldn't have done that."

"Are you really sorry?" Luke asked as he quickly assessed her face.

I stepped in to defend Emerson. "Luke, she said she's sorry. Can't we just drop this?"

"I am sorry," Em repeated.

"I need a favor," Luke replied, no longer making eye contact. "My little sister, she's twelve now. My dad and I don't really know how to shop for a twelve-year-old girl. I think she's getting picked on because she doesn't dress like the rest of the kids anymore. I need a girl to take her shopping."

Emerson sucked in a quick breath while I mentally added up just how close Luke's little sister and Pete would have been in age. Looking as pale as a ghost, she answered, "I'll do it."

Luke finally made eye contact with her. "Thanks, I'd appreciate it. And you're probably right about Eliza."

"We can go with you," I offered quickly. I had no idea how Emmy would handle doing something that an older sibling would do again.

"It would just embarrass her to be seen shopping with her brother. I got it under control." Her breathing had evened out and she looked much calmer than she'd appeared only moments before.

"So how are all those AP subjects coming, Matty?" Luke asked in a much needed abrupt topic change.

Groaning, I banged my head on the table. "I have to read, and there are no pictures. Even in the damn history book, there's not a single picture. Just words. Lots and lots of words."

"So it's going well then?" Luke asked with a laugh.

"Let me describe AP English and AP History to you. I go into the room for AP English, and all these kids who read for fun name drop every goddamn book they've ever read. And then the conversation of the nature of our existence begins. Some days they reach the conclusion that we exist and other days we live in a matrix or something. Who cares? We exist. Move on. Then, I go to AP History where the teacher walks around the room drilling us with questions. I think he's recently accepted that I'm a dumbass and lobs me easy questions now about who was president in the Civil War. And everyone else has to give a detailed response of what Jackson did or didn't do, and it took me about a week to figure out it was a different Jackson than the president." Defeated, I slumped against the table.

Emmy laughed. "I didn't tell you to join all of my classes."

"Not helpful, Em," I said with my head still down.

"Are the classes that bad, Em?" Luke asked. The bastard knew he was provoking me.

"No, not at all." Em took a bite of her apple. "I agree there are some oddballs in our AP English class and the teacher is a bit too 'let's talk about your emotions,' but her assignments are easy. And I don't mind the AP History class. Mr. Grayson is a really good teacher."

I groaned from my position.

"He's a little melodramatic," Emmy replied and ruffled my

hair. "Someone should have minded his own business and not demanded a seat next to me in every period."

"Wow, she figured out your plan, Sherlock." Luke laughed. "I wonder how she ever could have possibly figured out your near genius plan."

"I'm not in every class." I picked my head up. "I'm in a few of them."

"That's correct. He couldn't get into my all girl gym class or independent study," Emmy confirmed.

"Aim a softball at anyone's head these days?" Luke asked.

"Unfortunately, no. We're preparing for the state physical fitness test, and Mr. Rudolph separated me and Savannah into groups so that we would be on opposite ends of the gym at all times." Em tossed her apple core into the garbage a few feet away. "And can we not talk about Savannah while I am trying to eat? Even more preferable, we don't talk about her at all."

Sounded good to me.

Emerson

As promised, I drove up to the middle school a few days later to pick up Luke's little sister, Hannah, from school to take her shopping. It was a few minutes before the final bell, so I had a couple of minutes to lean against the car and wait. Other stood scattered around the parking lot waiting for their children to get out of school. The last day I had been here, I took final exams in every key subject to skip the last month of school and stay with Peter. I had rushed out of this place in a hurry, and Peter never made it to this school. It was one of a long list of things that Peter never got to do. Closing my eyes for a second, I took a deep breath. When I reopened them, I focused on the time that Matty decided to hoist a pair of boxers up the flagpole and the times we played tag after school until everyone was winded and laughing. By the time the bell rang, I had managed to calm myself on the outside. As I watched hundreds of kids swarm out of the school, I had no idea how I was supposed to find Hannah all of a sudden.

"Emerson?" I heard a tiny voice come from behind me.

Whipping around, I saw Hannah. Her strawberry-blonde hair was in a lopsided braid, her lip bumper made her lower lip jut out, and she was dressed in all purple except for her bright white tennis shoes. "Hannah." I smiled at her. Without warning, she ran up and hugged my waist. I squeezed her back even as another part of me cracked. Peter was the last kid to hug me. Blinking back my tears, I put an arm around her. "Are you ready to do some shopping?" She nodded and ran to the other side of my car. I know it sounds insane, but a small part of me felt like I was cheating on my little brother, and I couldn't fully wrap my head around letting another little kid into my life. I pushed the thoughts to the back of my mind and got into the car.

As I drove, I realized that Hannah didn't talk much. To be

more accurate, she didn't talk at all. "Do you want to go shopping, Hannah?" I asked, suddenly curious if this trip was what she wanted or Luke thought she needed. I was all too familiar with being on the wrong side of one those trips.

Glancing at her out of the corner of my eye, I saw her nod her head in affirmation. We didn't talk for the rest of the ride. I was wrong. Hannah was nothing like Peter and everything like me. Even if I couldn't pull myself out of the constant pain I felt, I was pretty sure I had the strength to pull my new mini me out of it.

When I parked the car, I turned to her. "Hannah, can I talk to you for a second?"

She nodded her head in acceptance. "Parents suck sometimes. My parents are wonderful examples of that. My parents are ridiculously smart, but they should never have been parents. It just wasn't in them to do it. Maybe they never knew how. I don't really know." I stopped speaking and looked at Hannah's eyes brimming with tears. "Your mom didn't leave because of anything you did or because you weren't good enough, Hannah. It's the other way around. Your mom left because she wasn't good enough, sweetie. I know it must be hard living with two boys, but they are good people. They love you so much, even if neither of them knows the first thing about braiding hair." I tugged on her braid gently.

"I miss my mom," Hannah cried quietly.

Reaching across the seat, I held her hand. "I know, Hannah." And I did know. I knew exactly what it felt like to be emotionally abandoned by your parents, but I also knew that sometimes no parent was better than a poor excuse for one.

After about ten minutes of crying, she wiped her eyes. Putting on a brave face, she asked, "Time to shop?"

"Absolutely."

We must have gone to at least seven different stores that afternoon. With the lovely swipe of my parents' credit card, I bought her a wardrobe that any seventh grader would be envious of: designer jeans, sweaters that accented her hair and eyes, shoes for every type of event, and a dress that made her look two years older. We agreed not to tell Luke about that last one. Once we finished shopping for clothes, I took her to get her ears pierced. I was hoping a guy worked at the stand, so I could flirt my way to getting her ears pierced. Technically, she couldn't sign for herself, and I shouldn't sign for her. When we arrived at the small jewelry store, I found Lexie and an older guy working there.

"Hey, Emerson," Lexie said kindly.

"Hey, Lex," I replied and pulled her to the side slightly. "I'm with Luke's little sister. Is there any way we can get her ears pierced?"

"She's supposed to have an adult sign for her," Lexie whispered.

"Can we pretend that I'm eighteen?" I asked in a hushed voice. "Her mom isn't around, and if Luke and his father are left up to this, it wouldn't occur to them until maybe her thirtieth birthday."

"Hey, Steve," Lex called out. "We have an ear piercing to do." She gestured at Hannah.

"Are you eighteen?" Steve asked me.

Propping myself against the counter so that he could see a decent way down my shirt, I replied, "Of course." Without looking back up at my face, he nodded and went to get the stuff for ear piercing.

I turned around to find Lexie laughing at me. "And what would Matt think?" Lexie asked, still giggling.

"That I'm resourceful?" I offered. "Come on, Lex, you can help Hannah and me find her first pair of earrings." I linked my arm through both girls and dragged them to look at the case of studs.

Hannah did really well getting her ears pierced; she only squeezed my arm once. I howled when I got my ears pierced.

After we bought a pair of studs and alcohol wipes to keep her ears from getting infected, we stopped at the food court. I bought both of us soft pretzels and drinks while she waited at a table where she stayed in my sight.

"Hannah, can I ask you a question?" I asked.

"Sure," she replied with a mouth full of pretzel.

"Why do you want to change the way you dress?" I wasn't necessarily a fan of her all purple wardrobe that looked like a tribute to Barney the Dinosaur, but I also didn't want her to be someone else if she actually was happy in the clothes.

"I hear the other kids make fun of my clothes, and I don't have a lot of friends," Hannah answered shyly.

"Hannah, I could and should tell you that it will get better and bullies will eventually get what is coming to them, but I know what matters to you is the right now. You will definitely be the best-dressed twelve-year-old girl after today, but you have to believe in yourself before anyone else can really do it. Be proud of who you are. You are a strong, beautiful, young woman who is kind and has an older brother who adores her. It matters what you look and feel like on the inside too, okay?" I knew right then and there that I had officially become the world's biggest hypocrite. Rather than being beautiful from the inside out, I hid behind my clothes and looks. Like I said before, I had drowned a long time ago from what I had seen and what I had done, but Hannah, she still had a chance if someone pushed her toward the shallow water again.

Matt

"Why do I have to memorize a whole bunch of dumb dates and names?" I asked dropping my book in frustration onto my lap. As was becoming a routine, I studied at Emmy's house on Sunday after we went for a run. Currently, I was lying on my back in her king-sized bed holding my AP History book.

"There's a test tomorrow?" Emmy replied. She was lying a foot or so away from me propped up on her elbows to read. We both knew she wasn't actually reading though. She was scanning information that would somehow stick with her until the day she died.

"Give me a five-minute nap and then wake me up, okay?" I rolled onto my side to face her. We had an established routine at this point. During school hours and social events, we were all over each other. Outside of that, we stayed on neutral topics like school. I had about a million other questions that I would rather ask her, but I was too afraid of pushing her away.

"What have you learned in the last hour?"

"Stonewall Jackson really loved his horse. Chamberlain's from Maine. He was a nerd. He won some medals for his swinging door tactic." I paused, fairly proud of myself. Clearly, I had made significant headway.

"That is what you got out of the last hour?" Em asked incredulously.

"That's more than I knew an hour ago," I replied, closing my eyes.

"Matty, you're going to fail this class." Em kicked me in the leg to get me to open my eyes back up.

"I think we all knew that was coming, right?" I, at least, had known when I transferred into AP English and AP History that my odds of passing both of them were pretty low. A trip to summer school wouldn't be the worst thing that ever happened to me.

"Why did you transfer into classes you knew you weren't going to pass? You would have had two classes with me anyway."

"Two wasn't enough," I replied simply. She had to have known that I would do anything for her, including failing the humanities.

"You can't fail History because of me."

"I'm not failing History because you. I am failing History because I am bad at History."

"I have an idea," Em said. "Go get your swimming trunks on."

"What?" I asked. "We're going for a swim?"

"Just go and put them on," Em shoved all her weight into mine to inch me off the bed.

I reluctantly walked next door, tossed on a pair of swim trunks, a T-shirt, and a sweatshirt. By the time I had returned, Em had lit both fireplaces on both sides of her back patio and had turned on all of the outside heaters. "Sit," Em ordered. "Give me one minute to go change and get our stuff."

Relaxing, I stretched out on a lounger near one of the fireplaces. Maybe she thought going for a swim would wake me up. I didn't have the heart to break it to her that we could do laps for an hour, and I wouldn't have enough energy to learn everything I needed to about the Civil War and the immediate aftermath.

When Em came back out, she was wearing a T-shirt and running shorts and carrying a stack of papers. "Here's the deal. I ask you a question. If you get it wrong, you have to jump into the water and pull yourself back out without using the steps. You keep going till you get one right, and then it's my turn." She dropped the stack of papers onto the table and stripped out of her T-shirt and running shorts. Her bright turquoise bikini stood out against the remnants of her summer tan and made her eyes even brighter. I didn't want to stare, but I did. She looked incredible. I knew she had a good body from all her shorts and tight clothing, but I didn't know that she had an incredible butt and well, let's just say, she had an incredible everything. "Matty, eyes back up. Your turn to strip, bud."

"Is there any chance you can wear this outfit for all future studying dates?" I asked as I tugged my T-shirt and sweatshirt over my head in one quick move. When I glanced over, I noticed she was staring at my abs. "Are you checking me out?"

"You are supposedly my boyfriend," she replied laughing. "Get to the other side of the pool, Romeo."

Begrudgingly, I trudged to the other side of the pool and grabbed a paper full of questions on my way. "Alright, first question." As she glanced down to read it, I took another glance at Emmy.

"I can feel you staring. Okay, easy one. Who was president following Lincoln?"

"Grant," I replied with a smug smile. "My turn." I searched the sheet for the hardest questions. "How many states formed the Confederacy before Lincoln was even inaugurated?"

"Seven. South Carolina, Georgia, Mississippi, Alabama, Florida, Louisiana, and Texas."

"Seriously, you know that?"

"Yes, and now you do too." She glanced down at her sheet of questions again. "Who was president of the Confederacy during the Civil War?"

"Robert E. Lee?" Who the hell knew the answer to that? The guy lost whoever it was. Even I had heard the quote about winners writing history.

"Dive in." Em gestured to the pool.

I dove into the pool easily and swam back up to the top. "Who was it?"

"Jefferson Davis," she replied. "Jefferson Davis was president of the Confederacy. She gestured for me to pull myself out of the pool which I did with little problem.

Over the course of the next three hours, I probably had to dive into the pool and heave myself about 50 goddamn times. Emmy went in exactly once, and I think she threw the question because she was getting bored and wanted to go for a swim. As I pulled my now aching muscles out of the pool for the last time, Emmy walked over to the towel warmer and tossed me a beach towel. "I think you are good to go for the test tomorrow, Matty." She wrapped a beach towel around herself and sank onto the large lounger near one of the fireplaces.

"Thanks, coach." I walked over to the towel warmer, grabbed another towel, and then headed to the lounger to lie down next to her. As I sank into the warm seat heated by the fire and wrapped both of us in the extra towel, she nestled herself against me. Two and a half years ago, this wouldn't have been a big deal whatsoever. In fact, I'm pretty sure she used me as her personal headrest for the first 14 years of our lives, but now, it felt like a huge step forward with Emmy. I put my arm out, and she pulled in closer as she draped her arm across my chest and laid her head on my shoulder. Under the nice warm towels, I rubbed her back. "Thanks for helping me study," I whispered and kissed her forehead.

"Thanks for being a good pillow," she responded sleepily. Two steps forward, and one step back.

Emerson

"Okay, class, today we're going to discuss how Holden in *Catcher in the Rye* compares to Anna in *My Sister's Keeper*. Specifically, we want to look at the similarities and differences in how they react to and cope with their siblings having cancer." Mrs. Ferguson stood in front of the class, holding both books in front her. On the inside, I groaned. First of all, I highly doubted there was going to be a question about cancer on the AP test. Mrs. Ferguson could sell her touchy, feely shit to someone else. I prepared myself to tune out for the remainder of the period. Next to me, Matt shifted uncomfortably. He knew I didn't want to listen to this dumb discussion; thankfully, he passed the AP History test with a B and was still keeping his head above water.

"Lexie, what do you think?" Mrs. Ferguson asked.

"I don't think there is a right way or wrong way to deal with the loss of a sibling, Mrs. Ferguson." In my head, I gratefully accepted her answer. I knew Lexie was giving me a break; she was the closest thing I had to an actual girl friend.

"I think Holden blames all of his problems on his brother's death when really he was just as much a phony as everyone else he put into that category," a kid whose name I hadn't bothered to learn piped up from the other side of the room. I clutched my notebook until my knuckles turned white.

"His younger brother died," Matty replied as he shot a look of death toward the back of the classroom. "Holden put his hand through a window because he was so upset. Cut the guy a break." Wow, Matty actually read the book or SparkNotes. Either way, he read something.

"He was mentally ill and used his brother's death as a scapegoat," the kid shot back.

"Was that in the book?" Lexie answered. "Can you point to a passage where it says that or that is even implied? Quit playing psychiatrist, Walter." Walter seemed to be a fitting name for this curmudgeon of a kid who was a pseudo-intellectual.

Another girl with glasses entered the conversation. "People die every day, Lexie. That doesn't give someone free rein to do what they want."

"Please tell me the proper way to grieve." I turned around in my desk to stare down Walter and Specs. "Better yet, do you two have siblings?"

Both nodded their head.

"Are they still alive?" I demanded.

Again, both nodded their head.

"Then, please tell me what makes you experts on dealing with siblings' deaths." I was on fire now. Mrs. Ferguson couldn't have stopped me even if she tried.

"You don't need to be an expert to know Holden's annoying," Specs answered me. I had already decided that I wasn't going to waste time learning her name.

"If we're just making opinionated statements now, then I don't need to be an expert to know your British accent is phony." I had completely twisted in my seat to glare.

"Emerson!" Mrs. Ferguson interjected. Matt tried to redirect the conversation. "Mrs. Ferguson, maybe you should ask a less opinionated question if you don't want opinions for answers."

"I don't need your help teaching, Matthew," Mrs. Ferguson snapped at him. "Let's move to *My Sister's Keeper*. Is Anna a more sympathetic narrator?"

"I think so," Specs answered. Seriously, was this the only student who talked in the class?

"Why do you think she is more sympathetic?" Mrs. Ferguson asked.

"Because she was continually forced to undergo unnecessary operations, and her parents used her as a constant guinea pig for her sister," Specs answered, sitting back in her seat clearly proud of her dumb answer.

"That's not the point of the book," I replied, rolling my eyes. "Anna's selfishness about donating her kidney is a red herring for the fact that Kate didn't want to go through any more operations. It was a simple plot twist to throw readers off in terms of what was really happening. Anna's redeeming quality is that she knowingly follows Kate's wishes even though it's killing her on the inside and tearing her family apart. Even though Anna doesn't want to, Anna lets Kate go on her own terms."

"Morally, it was wrong what they did to Anna. You can't create or destroy babies just in hopes of keeping another kid alive. If someone dies, it's God's plan," a girl sitting behind Specs said quietly. The girl wore a skirt to her ankles and a turtleneck with a cross hanging around her neck. Lovely, the religious zealot was joining the conversation.

"It's a piece of fiction," Lexie answered quickly. "How can we possibly talk about God's plan in a fictional piece of literature?" I appreciated Lexie's effort, but I was going for the jugular at this point.

"First of all, a baby was not destroyed in the book. It was created, so we can drop the baby murdering argument. Second, what gives you the right to say that a life in a womb is more important than a life already being lived? Do we not have any responsibility to the people who are in this world already?" I could feel myself heating up as I got further into the debate.

"Unborn babies can't fight for themselves. We have to do it for them," replied my new friend, the zealot.

"Are you going to show me pictures of babies in the womb or aborted babies now?" I asked, once again rolling my eyes. "Isn't that about where we are in this class, which has apparently turned into religion? Children with cancer can't fight for themselves either. These are kids who are already in this world who are suffering with an affliction they didn't ask for. And you show me a God who thinks making living breathing children suffer is right or the grand plan, and I'll show you a God who is actually cruel and vicious."

The zealot gasped and her eyes filled with tears. To be honest, I didn't even care. I was fed up with the conversation that had nothing to do with English and everything to do with uneducated opinions. From behind me, Lex patted my shoulder. Gratefully, the bell rang before round three could begin.

"Emerson, please stay after class," Mrs. Ferguson stated, looking highly irritated.

After everyone left the room, I turned to face my English teacher.

"Emerson, this class is a safe zone, and I think you owe some people an apology. You got very personal in your attacks."

"Mrs. Ferguson, if you want to punish me, give me a detention. This subject matter is personal, and there is no way I am apologizing to a bunch of people who stated their feelings on a topic they know nothing about. If you want to stay away from these conversations, then come up with a lesson plan that will teach us rhetorical devices and nonfiction. That is on the AP test, right?" I waited a second. "If you'd like me to go speak to the principal about what happened in class today, I would be more than happy to tell him about the lack of educational value to today's lesson." Once again, I knew I was crossing a line, but Mrs. Ferguson drew the freaking line by asking about our feelings on touchy subjects.

"You may go, Emerson," Mrs. Ferguson replied coldly. "I see you are nothing like your brother."

"Which one, Mrs. Ferguson? My older sibling or the one who died of leukemia at age seven?" I turned and left the classroom.

Matt

After English, Emmy didn't say a word through all of our morning classes. Personally, I wanted to kick their asses. Realistically, I couldn't ever hit one of the girls, but I did have good ole' Walt in my gym class. With any luck, dodgeball would be on the agenda soon. When we sat down at our lunch table and Em still hadn't spoken a word, I was worried. A ranting and yelling Em was better than a seething Em.

Out of nowhere, Lexie plopped down across from us. "Are you okay?" Lexie asked facing Em directly. In one minute, Lexie had been able to ask the question that I had been wanting to ask for the past three hours.

"I'm fine," Em answered as if it was a reflex.

"No, you're not," Lexie pushed. "I am freaking pissed, so there is no way you can be 'fine,' Em."

As Luke sat down, Em spoke again. "Okay, I'm irate. I had to spend forty minutes of my life listening to Zealot and Specs discuss cancer and life as if they have any idea of what it's like to watch your sibling waste away from it. If you want me to be honest, I've been hoping all morning that one of their siblings wakes up with leukemia tomorrow. That's how freaking pissed I am right now."

"What happened?" Luke asked.

"A few idiots in our English class decided they had all the answers when it came to cancer and how to grieve for a sibling," I replied. "I'm a dumbass, and I know their answers were out of line."

"Not according to Mrs. Ferguson." Em shredded a napkin in her lap while she spoke. "Mrs. Ferguson thinks I owe them all an apology for getting personal."

"Are you serious?" Lexie asked.

"Yes." Em shredded quicker.

"What did you say?" I asked.

"I told her that she was going to have to give me a detention because there is no way that I would ever apologize, and I was more than happy to go talk to the principal about what she allowed to happen in the classroom today." Em looked up unhappily.

"If you get a detention for what happened in class today, I will go to the principal," Lexie replied. I didn't know Lexie well in grade school or now even, but I was glad that Em had made a friend who seemed to have her back.

"Sorry, Em," Luke replied looking sincerely apologetic. Ever since she had taken his sister shopping, Luke had gone out of his way to be more polite to Emmy.

"It's fine," Emmy replied again though she clearly wasn't fine.

"Let's talk about something fun," Luke switched the topic. "My dad is going out of town over New Year's and my little sister is sleeping over a new friend's house which means empty house for Lucas." I kept forgetting that winter break was just a few days away. Unfortunately, I would spend most of it out of town on my family's annual ski trip. I wasn't looking forward to any of it. I didn't want to leave Em by herself on her first Christmas at home away from Peter, and I was terrified that a good burst of wind or snow would kill Mallory.

"Are you having a party?" Em asked.

"No, I'm having selective people over for the night. Girls wear dresses. Guys wear button downs. All the alcohol you can drink. People can stay the night."

"Who are the lucky individuals who will be spending New Year's Eve at your house?" I asked. I actually couldn't wait to hear the answer; if you asked almost any person in the school, he or she would tell you that Luke was a great friend. I didn't even really have a clue which ones he considered actual friends.

"You, Em, Eliza, Tyler, and Lexie." He turned to Lexie. "That is assuming you want to come?"

"I'm in," Lexie replied easily.

"How are you going to separate Eliza and Savannah on a party night?" Em asked.

"Savannah's family goes to the Caribbean for the entirety of break, so she won't even be in town."

"Why only the six of us?" I asked as I considered the very random list.

"Well, dumbass, you're my best friend. Em is your girlfriend, and I've known her forever. I'm secretly dating Eliza. I owe Tyler for all of the booze he's supplied me in the past three years, and Lexie is Em's friend, so she's one of us now. And I don't want a bunch of people I'm marginally friends with destroying the house." Luke spelled it out fairly simply.

"I'm in," Em confirmed.

"Yeah, man, me too," I agreed.

"Great, Eliza and Tyler have already agreed. It's going to be a kickass party." Luke looked pleased with himself.

Emerson

Christmas came before I knew it. My brother took the day off, so I wouldn't be home alone. I appreciated his considerations, but I spent my last two Christmas eating in front of a turned off television. We had set up and decorated a tree and bought each other unnecessary gifts, but to be honest, it all felt wrong without Pete. When Brad was away at college, Peter and I were in charge of decorating the tree. It was miraculous any decorating got accomplished given the facts that Peter just liked eating the popcorn and I just wanted to belt out Christmas tunes. For Peter's last Christmas, we somehow had left over lights and strands of beads. Not wanting them to go to waste, Peter wrapped Matty and me up together in the strands and lights. We waddled out to the front porch, and Peter plugged in the lights. I had never seen Peter laugh so hard in his life. Somehow Matty freed one of his arms so he could do the robot and stuff when cars passed the house. My holidays went from laughter and lights to an unwelcome reminder of what once was.

As I forced myself out to the kitchen Christmas morning, I could hear Brad speaking quietly on the phone. I stomped my feet a little louder so he could hear me coming; I didn't want to invade his privacy. When I turned the corner of the bend to enter the kitchen, Brad looked up at me quickly. As I poured myself some juice and grabbed a granola bar, he quickly got off the phone.

"You could have talked," I said with a mouthful of granola.

"Merry Christmas to you too," he replied.

"Merry Christmas, Bradley. Who was on the phone? New girlfriend?" I asked hopefully. Even if I wasn't happy, I wanted to see my older brother in a happy and healthy relationship. He deserved that.

"It was our parents." He looked at me for some kind of reaction.

"I didn't know you still talked to them." I stared down at my juice. Realistically, I knew Brad always had a better relationship with them than I did, but I hoped he would pick me.

"Today was the first time I talked to them since signing the legal guardian forms and paperwork for you. They just wanted to wish us a Merry Christmas." He stabbed his fork in the omelet in front of him.

"Us or you, Brad?" I rolled my eyes. "I've lived with them the last two years, and they never once wished me a Merry Christmas." They were always too busy saving someone else's life to notice that they had essentially lost two children of their own.

When he didn't reply immediately, I knew the answer. I let out a sigh. "Really, it's okay. I didn't expect anything else."

"I'm sorry, Emerson."

"For what? Still talking to them or continuing to play their favorite? They left Peter to die in that hospital bed alone. How can you possibly forgive them?"

"Emerson, there are some things you don't understand." Like hell, I didn't understand. I had sat in the room with Peter the whole time, and it was my butt that got tossed on a plane to France without a thought of what they were doing to me.

"Like what, Bradley? That our parents still speak to you? That our parents didn't pay one iota of attention to me for two years in France? That they let Peter cry for them so they could go help other people's families? Seriously, what piece of the puzzle am I missing?" My eyes filled with tears because I was so angry, but I would never cry one tear over either of them for the rest of my life.

"Emerson, they talk to me because I'm exactly who they wanted me to be. You took the road less traveled, and they didn't know how to handle it."

"Just because I didn't live up to their expectations, it was okay for them to basically treat me as an annoying house guest?"

"Do you remember when you took that IQ Test when you were eight or nine?"

"What does that have to do with anything?" I was pissed, and he wanted to talk about IQ tests?

"You scored over a one hundred and sixty, which far surpassed any score I had ever put on the board. You fell in the highly gifted to profoundly gifted range. Our parents were ecstatic. It was as though you inherited the absolute best of both of their intelligences. When they tried to talk to you about it, you laughed."

"I was freaking eight years old!" I yelled.

"Emerson, they already had brochures picked out for the most prestigious boarding schools and private schools. They were ready to put you on an accelerated cycle and give you every kind of tutor and privilege their money could buy. And you didn't want any part of it. When they tried to reason with you, you jumped in the pool with a sundress on and sat on the bottom blowing bubbles up at them." I vaguely remembered them standing on the edge of the pool until my mother stomped off. I didn't surface till they left. I thought my lungs were going to explode because I stayed under so long.

"I was eight, Brad. They wanted to change my whole life."

"Yes, and at eight years old, I was already doing everything they wanted, Emerson. If they wanted me to enter a competition, I entered. If they wanted all As, I gave them all As. They didn't know what to do when you came into the picture and did exactly what you wanted whether it coincided with their wishes or not. They didn't know how to raise you, especially when you were actually brighter than they could have imagined and you wanted nothing to do with it."

"I was their daughter. They were supposed to love me unconditionally."

"They do, Emerson."

"Don't patronize me, Brad. We both know the terms of this

arrangement. For once in your life, call a spade a spade. Quit being Switzerland." I glared at him. I had never been angrier at Brad in my life. "And what was Peter's grand sin? What did he do to be cast out with me? He never made it to the IQ test."

"Pete loved you more than them from the second he opened his eyes. Even as a baby, he would scream until you picked him up and rocked him to sleep. You weren't just his big sister. You were Peter's everything. They never had a fighting chance with him."

"So it's my fault that they wouldn't sit in the room with Peter as he died? He asked for them, Brad. He asked for his MOTHER and FATHER!"

"They should have been there for him, Em. I honestly believe they didn't know how. Emotions were never really their strong spot. They had to blame themselves for Peter's death. They were doctors who couldn't save their own son."

"You can rationalize them however you want. In fact, I don't even hate them for not loving me." I paused to put together my thoughts. "I can accept the fact that I didn't behave like the daughter that they would have liked to have. Peter though, I will never forgive them for letting him cry for them when he was so scared already. Never." I wiped a tear away from my cheek as I talked about my little brother. "They are monsters who let their youngest son die believing that they didn't love him. And the fact that you can forgive them for that—" I gulped in more air. "The fact that you can just forgive them for everything assures me that you are your parents' son."

"Emerson."

"No, I'll be in my room till you leave for your night shift. Please don't speak to me." I walked back toward my room, locked the door, and crawled under the covers. I was officially alone. Coming home wasn't all that different from being in France after all. I knew then that I was going to take all of the sedatives I had stashed as soon as Brad left for work. Feeling comforted because I knew I wasn't going to be alive much longer, I let myself drift into a deep sleep.

Sitting on my bed bored, I painted my fingernails bright red. My parents would say a 13-year-old was too young to have red fingernails, but I was banking on the fact that they wouldn't notice. I might even be able to get a tattoo without them noticing. As I thought over what I would want drawn on my body for life, I heard the sounds of things falling coming from down the hall.

Interested in what Peter was up to, I went bounding down the hall. Most of the time you hear about how teenagers don't want to deal with their six-year-old brothers, or at least most of my friends seemed to hate their younger siblings. I felt the opposite. Even on days when he was trying to annoy me, I found it funny because the look of concentration on his face was so intense. As I entered his room, I saw Peter halfway in his closet feverishly digging for something.

"What are you doing, Peter Rabbit?" I asked leaning against his door jam.

"I have to find a shoebox and decorate it," Peter responded solemnly. And then he went straight back to digging.

I walked into his room and sat on his bed. "Peter, why do you need to decorate a shoebox?" We were out of school for summer, so it couldn't possibly have anything to do with homework.

Without even pulling his head out of the closet, he answered me. "I found a dead bird on the porch, and I want to bury it." The seriousness of his voice made me laugh. "It's not funny, Em."

Forcing myself to maintain a straight face, I thought over his burial. Immediately, touching a dead bird grossed me out, and I tried to think of ways out of it. "Some other animal has probably come for it. You know the Lion King and the circle of life, right? It's probably gone." I didn't want to burst his bubble, but I also didn't want to bury a bird.

"I put an empty flower pot over it, so it would safe until it was time to bury it." He triumphantly stood up from his closet with a shoebox in it. "Now, we just have to find decorations and give the bird a name," he said taking stock of his room.

"What is this 'we' business? Seriously, Peter, I think we should just toss it or let another animal take care of it." What if the thing was already decaying? Yikes. I didn't want to find out.

"Emmy, it's a bird and it's by himself." Peter looked at me as though this was a sufficient enough answer. "He died alone, but we should at least bury him so that he knows his bird life will be missed." I started to wonder if maybe we shouldn't have taken Peter to our grandparents' funeral last year.

Realizing I'd lost the battle, I stood up. "Well then, let's go bury a bird." One hour later, we had one of the most hideously decorated shoeboxes. Peter kept putting stickers everywhere and drawing pictures of other birds while I mainly wrote song lyrics in nail polish. When we were done, I shoveled a hole for Peter in the side yard. I forced him to put on gloves before he picked up the dead bird and gently laid it to rest in its tissue box coffin.

After Peter placed the box in the ground, he began the funeral in a sad tone. "Thank you to all those who came today. I'm sure Oscar, the bird, would be glad to see you." My little brother watched a lot of Sesame Street when he was younger. "Oscar, we are lucky to have your chirping and to have seen you flying gracefully in the sky. As you soar up to heaven, please know that you will be missed." I stood stupefied by younger brother. There were days where he behaved like a rambunctious six-year-old, and then there were days like today when he seemed like a very old soul trapped in a kid's body. Peter dutifully covered the box in the ground. He made a little cross with stones near the side of the house where the bird was laid to rest.

"Hey, Peter, how do you know that you've heard that exact bird chirp or seen that exact bird fly before?" I asked, genuinely curious.

"Does it really matter?" Peter asked as he walked to the garage with the shovel. "I don't need to know every person alive in the world to know that to someone that person's life is the most important." Taking the shovel off him, I leaned down to hug him, dead bird gloves and all.

"To me, Pete, your life will always be the most important." I hugged my little brother tightly.

"Then don't do it, okay? Em, promise me you won't do it." Before I had a chance to ask him what he was talking about, he was abruptly pulled away from me.

I woke breathing hard and sitting straight up in my bed. I hadn't dreamed of Peter in a while. Hazily, I started to piece the dream back together. The memory was real. Peter did insist we bury a dead bird, but the last thing he said to me never happened. When I told that his life would always be the most important, he just hugged me back. He never said anything.

Getting out of bed, I walked to the mirror in my bathroom. The bottle of pills and the water sat waiting for me. Picking up the glass, I dumped the water into the sink and returned the stash of pills to the back of one of the bathroom drawers.

"Peter, I don't know how to do this without you." Letting myself slide down the bathroom wall, I put my head into my hands and cried.

Matt

Being away from Emerson for an entire week was almost paralyzing me; I don't know how I went two years without her. My parents, who I think watched a little too much Full House with us when we were younger, were big believers in family bonding over the holidays and no technology usage. On the bright side, I was finally back home and Mallory had survived the family trip. She didn't ski which was probably for the best. Even now on New Year's Eve, Mallory was curled up in her room with old pictures of her and Cole and old home movies. As I buttoned my last button on my black shirt, I dug for Em's present under my bed. I bought it a while ago, and finally, I had an excuse to give it to her.

Instead of going to her front door this time, I cut through my back yard and hers to let myself in through the back gate. Glancing at the pool that helped me pass a History exam, I walked to the back door to her bedroom and knocked lightly. After a few seconds, I started to worry that she was waiting for me in the front of the house. Things were a whole hell of a lot easier when I could just burst into her room or house unannounced. Just as I was about to give up and head for the front of the house, her back door swung open.

Em stood in the door in three-inch black heels and a short, black, lace dress that had lace running up her one arm while the other arm remained exposed as the black dress sliced diagonally across the upper part of her chest to reach the sleeve. With her blonde hair pulled into a styled ponytail and a slash of dark red lipstick across her mouth, she looked absolutely breathtaking.

"Emerson, you look beautiful." I reached out gently to pull her into a hug. Seeing how she looked, I was ecstatic that we were going to a house with only two other guys. The guys in our school already thought she was hot; in fact, I threatened to kick some guy's ass if he didn't quit talking about her body one day in the locker room.

"Welcome home, Matty," she whispered in my ear as she hugged me back. She didn't know it, but I was at home finally with her. She had always been my home since the day she was born.

I tugged her gently into the bedroom with me and shut the door behind me. "I have been waiting to give you your Christmas gift for like a month now." We both sat down on her bed. Reaching into my pocket, I pulled out the small robin's egg blue box.

"Matt, I don't think I can accept that. I know how much stuff in those blue little boxes cost." She eyed the box hesitantly.

"Well, I've had two and a half years of missed birthdays and holidays to save up. So let's just say happy fifteenth and sixteenth birthday in addition Happy Easter and Merry Christmas." I took her hand that was resting in her lap and opened it gently to place the box in her palm.

She undid the ribbon as if it was the most important gift she had ever received and gently lifted open the box. "Matt—"

"Wait," I interrupted her. "At least let me explain before you say you don't want it. I do love you, Em. I think I will always be in love with you. And I am certain that the guy in the picture in the locket will always love you too."

Hesitantly, Em opened the locket in the case. Inside, I had put two pictures of Peter. In the first, he was just a happy toddler. It was the first time we had ever taken him to a pond. We took turns holding him in a foot of water. Every time, a school of fish floated past our ankles, Peter had reached for them laughing. For some reason, that kid had a thing for fish since the moment he saw them. The second picture was one of the last pictures taken of him. For his last birthday, Em insisted on buying him an aquarium. The two of us went to every pet store in town. At the time, I whined that I was missing valuable time practicing soccer.

It was all worth it though. When he walked into his room and saw the fish tank, he practically flew to it. His smile in the picture was huge. It was Peter at his happiest. Em studied the picture carefully.

"Now, he'll always be with you. In your heart and above it. And hopefully, I get a place there too one day." I let out the huge breath I had been holding the entire time.

"Matty, this locket is the best gift anyone's ever given me. Thank you so much. I don't even know how to tell you how much this means to me," she finally replied as her eyes glistened with tears. I reached out to wipe the tear before it slid down her cheek and pulled her closer to me. She kissed my cheek sweetly and then laughed at the lipstick kiss she had left on me. Pulling my face closer to hers, she wiped away the lipstick gently with her thumb. "Will you put the locket on me?" Em asked.

"Sure, turn around." As she held her hair to one side, I clasped the locket around her neck. She stood up to examine it in the mirror. "It's beautiful, Matty. And luckily, Santa Claus left a present here for you too." She reached into her vanity and pulled out a small box. Walking back to the bed, she handed it to me.

"You didn't have to," I replied as she set the box on my knee.

"Neither did you, but we both did."

Unwrapping the box, I wondered what she could have possibly gotten me for Christmas. When I opened the box, I saw the nicest watch I had ever seen in my life.

"When you were little, you always stole your dad's watch, and he would get so pissed and chase you around the house." Em smiled at the memory. "I figured it was time you have your own."

"It's awesome," I replied, pulling it out. Em was right. I had always wanted one of those watches that told the time in like three different locations.

"Matt?" Em tugged on my arm. "I'm not ready to say the words because I don't know how to love anymore. If I could, it would be you." She gently took the watch out and flipped it over so I could see the inscription: M.E. When Em had learned how to spell at like age three, she was amazed that our first initials spelled a word. She told me that it made us more special.

"I'll wait." I smiled slowly at her. I kissed the tip of her nose. Nodding her head, she glanced down shyly. "Do you want to head over to Luke's?"

"Yes!" She smiled and touched her locket again. "I have all my stuff packed up for the night." She gestured to her bag packed by the door.

"Let's do this." I grabbed her bag in one hand and tucked her into my other arm as we headed out the door.

Emerson

After Matty gave me the locket and told me he loved me, there was no way I could tell him the truth. There was no way he would look at me the same way again. Maybe with pity. Disappointment. Or disgust. But he would never look at me as though I was the most important person in his life. And he certainly wouldn't still love me; he didn't even know the person he loved. Even though it frustrated me sometimes that Matty didn't acknowledge how much I'd changed, he was the only person who still thought that highly of me. Selfishly, I wasn't ready to let that go.

"Hey, are you okay?" Matty interrupted my thoughts.

"Yes, what do you think it's going to be like at Luke's?" I asked, feeling ridiculous in my dress. Lucas had better have appreciated my willingness to humor him.

"You know Luke. He will get everyone wasted one way or another." Matty ran his hand through his hair. "To be honest, I have no idea why we're going other than the fact that it's Luke, and he's convincing."

I laughed because I knew it was the truth. Luke could talk someone who lived on a tundra into buying more ice. "At least it's not a big group of people I don't know or do know and don't like."

As he pulled into Luke's driveway behind the other cars, he leaned over to kiss me. "Let's see if you're still saying that tomorrow." He grabbed both of our bags out of the back seat and led me up the steps to Luke's front door. Not bothering to knock, he swung the door open.

"Awww, it's my favorite couple." Luke walked over to greet us. I shrugged out of my jacket and tossed it on a coat rack. "Shit man, Emerson got really hot."

"You are going to get knocked on your ass if you keep

commenting on it," Matt replied.

"Well, this is fun so far." I squeezed between both of them. "Is everyone else here?"

"Kitchen," Luke replied, leading the way.

We were the last two to arrive. Everyone else stood around the food and counter with a cup in front of them. Eliza wore a short black dress that showed off how toned she was from cheerleading. If I had her arm muscles, I would never wear sleeves again. Lex went for a little more casual black dress; it hugged her cleavage and waist but then flared out slightly at the hips. It wasn't quite as short as mine or Eliza's.

"Em, you look hot," Lex shouted as she noticed me.

"Thanks, but you and Eliza should take a look in the mirror. You both look amazing in those dresses."

"Thanks," Eliza replied. She and I could probably never fully be friends because of the Savannah factor, but we were doing much better at polite conversation.

"What about me, Emerson?" Tyler asked. He gave his best model walk. "Do I look hot?"

"Not as good as Matt," I replied with a smile. Matt hugged me from behind.

"Will you two just get a room already?" Luke asked as he rolled his eyes.

"Are you offering yours?" I asked innocently.

"He's going to need his tonight," Eliza chimed in. "What do we want to do?"

"Dance party!" Lexie and I screamed at the same time. The three guys all sighed in mutual pain. Matty was not the world's worst dancer, but I preferred to dance with Lex and even Eliza. Dancing was just more fun with other girls. Begrudgingly, Luke went and set up party music.

"At least we'll have a good show," Tyler offered.

"That's what I'm concerned about, ass." Matt shoved him lightly.

"Shots first," Luke said, doling out the alcohol. We all tossed them back in unison.

"Let's dance on the counter," Eliza yelped as a popular song began to play. Following her lead, Lexie and I both kicked off our heels and swung ourselves up onto the counter. The guys watched as we goofed around dancing and singing. We stayed up there for three songs. Luke snapped pictures, and Tyler and Matt helped themselves to another shot.

When the third song ended and I realized that I was probably giving all of the guys a view up my skirt, I leaned down to step off the counter. Before I could swing my legs out, Matty lifted me off and kissed me. For the first time, I let go when we were kissing. I let myself enjoy the feel of his lips and body against mine. I pushed myself closer to him.

Matty let out a groan. "I'm going to need a room soon if you keep doing that," he whispered into my ear.

"Drinking game?" Tyler asked as he poured mixed drinks into cups for the six of us.

"What are we playing?" Eliza asked, hopping off the counter.

"Never Have I Ever?" Luke suggested.

"Works for me." Lex took a seat.

All six of us sat down at the table. Eliza sat to my left and Matt sat at my right. "Who's going first?" I asked.

"I will," Lex replied. "Never have I ever had sex." Wow, we were starting the game at the hard stuff. It was about then that I realized how bad things could get if I answered honestly. Lexie eyed the five of us.

Tyler, Eliza, Luke, Matt, and I all took a drink. Matt looked at me with a question on his face, and I looked away.

"Wow, all my friends are sluts," Lexie replied. "Tyler, you're up."

"Never have I ever switched all my classes to stalk a girl," Tyler said laughing.

"Screw you, Tyler." Matt picked up his drink once again.

"Your turn, Matthew," Tyler responded still laughing.

"Never have I ever hustled someone with a bet on flip cup," Matt said, giving both Tyler and me a look.

As we took our respective sips, Luke complained about losing his fifty dollars. I didn't know what Tyler put in these drinks, but they were strong even for me. I could feel a buzz starting. Since it was now my turn, I announced, "Never have I ever cheated on a test." I had very few options in this game. With mine, Luke, Tyler, and Eliza all raised their glasses.

"My turn!" Eliza announced happily. "Never have I ever smoked weed." Lexie, Luke, and I all picked up our cups. Once again, I could feel Matt staring at me as I took the drink. I had decided I was going to play honestly, and I had a feeling I had a lot more drinking in front of me. At least if I was drinking, I didn't actually have to say everything aloud. Liquid courage.

"I'm up." Luke thought for a second and then eyed Eliza who was already almost at the wasted mark. She was so small that it wasn't going to take much to put her under the table. "Never have I ever had sex in my parents' bed." Eliza pouted and reached for her cup; unfortunately, I also reached for mine.

"Seriously, Emerson?" Luke asked.

"Yes," I replied quickly, not daring to look at Matt. "Lexie's turn or we could play another game."

"I'll go," Lexie winked at me. "Never have I ever played varsity soccer."

"Weak," Tyler commented, but threw his free hand around the back of her chair as he reached for his drink again. Matt and Luke followed suit.

"Never have I ever failed my driver's test three times." Tyler took his turn. Both Lexie and Luke were forced to drink on that one.

"Faulty driving testers," Luke commented, after he took his swig.

"I'm sure, Maverick." Tyler laughed at Lexie whose face

turned red with her second drink. "What about the three car accidents?"

"Learning experiences in life," Luke replied dismissively.

"Back to me, huh?" Matt glanced around the table. "Never have I ever snorted coke."

"Dumbass, you have to drink if no one at the table has done it." Luke reached across the table to shove Matt's glass closer to him.

"He doesn't have to drink," I said quickly. "I do." And I took another large gulp of the alcohol.

"You've snorted coke, Emerson?" Matty asked. Given that he rarely used my full name, I knew where this was headed.

"Yeah, I have." I took another sip just because I suddenly felt like I was being interrogated with bright lights.

"When did you start doing drugs?" Matt pushed. And I suddenly felt very drunk and once again very alone.

"Matt, back off of her," Luke demanded. Tears threatened to splash my cheeks, but I blinked them back.

"Christ, have you been on drugs since you've been back?" The accusation in his voice was so heavy that I felt like I'd been slapped. "It would explain some things."

"Matt, back the hell off," Lexie said, this time as she glared at him across the table.

"I've spent the past two years 'backing the hell off" her and look where that's got us?" Matt yelled back. "Come on, Emerson, you drank a lot during that game, what the hell have you been up to?" As he yelled, Lexie scooted her chair between mine and Matt's, and Tyler put an arm across Matt to hold him back in the chair.

"Why does no one else have to explain themselves and I have to defend what I have done?" I asked. My voice cracked in the middle of the sentence.

"She's right," Eliza said softly. "The rest of us didn't explain our drinks. She shouldn't have to explain hers."

"The rest of us haven't snorted coke," Matt fired back at her.

"Oh screw you, Matt." Eliza shook her head. "Do you ever get tired of being so self-righteous?"

"At least I'm not afraid of my goddamn best friend," Matt said, staring directly at Eliza.

"No, you only abandon yours." Eliza gestured to me with a shrug of her shoulder.

"Will everyone please stop?" I whispered. Holding my head in my hands, I took in a deep breath. "I'll answer the question."

"Before she answers the question, no one talks about it once we leave here." Luke sent daggers at everyone. "Got it? Whatever the hell she says, stays in this house." Everyone at the table gave a slight nod except Matty. Reaching behind my neck, I unclasped the necklace Matty had just given me and rested it gently on the table.

"The day of Peter's funeral? I didn't know my parents had plane tickets ready for less than an hour after we put my little brother into the ground. I just wanted to stay at the grave. Peter was the best part of the Caulfield family, and he was gone so quickly. I knew he was sick, but you hear people talk about fighting cancer for years. I didn't know that my brother's fight was over before it had even begun. I didn't tell him everything I needed to say, and my parents just shoved me on a plane with them because I was a minor and they had numerous job offers from prestigious hospitals all over France." I had tears streaming down my face; I didn't even know I was crying. For that moment, I was back on the plane that was taking me far away from my little brother.

"Are you really going to blame everything on Peter's death?" Matty interrupted me. "You know he would have never been okay with what you did."

"Matt, I swear to God, I will kick your ass myself if you don't shut up," Lexie whispered as she grabbed my hand.

"It's okay. He's right. Peter would hate the person I've

become." A small sob escaped despite my best efforts to hold back. "I didn't do anything the first two years we were there. Instead of enrolling me in a school, my parents had tutors brought in to keep me on track. My parents pushed the tutors to test me further, but I wouldn't jump through the hoops they kept setting up for me. I spent the majority of my time there alone and missing Peter so much that I thought I would actually die." As I told the story, I saw the revolving doors of tutors who came through those two years. At first, they all tried to push me to reach my potential; eventually, I told all of them that they could literally sit and do nothing, and I would still pass the test. And that's what they did. They told my parents I refused to move at a quicker pace. My parents didn't even talk to me about it; they communicated their demands through the tutor. I pulled myself away from the memories to continue. "The only person I kept in touch with while I was there was Brad. He knew I was absolutely miserable and alone. For some reason, I thought if I could back to our house and Peter's grave, it would help."

"I sent you a lot of e-mails, Emerson. You never answered one of them." Matt searched my eyes. Unfortunately, he was searching for the one thing I was devoid of: the capability of being the Emerson he knew.

"I know that. I read some of them, but it was hard on me to hear from you. It was like rubbing salt into a wound of everything I'd lost in the past year. And if you were going to move on, you needed to do so without me in the picture. Judging from my return, you did move on without me. You had a perfectly normal teenage life with soccer and Savannah, and you were doing fine."

"How the hell do you know how I felt? You made a decision that affected both of us without even asking what I wanted." Matt hadn't taken his eyes off of me. It wasn't exactly looks of love he was shooting in my direction.

"You don't always get a choice or a vote, Matty. I certainly didn't. If you're asking me if I regret my decision to not respond to you, I don't. You can say whatever you want, but you grew up to be everything you wanted. Star soccer player. Decent student. Cheerleader for a girlfriend."

"What changed your parents' mind about letting you come back?" Eliza asked. Maybe it would be better if I faced her for this part of the story. Her judgment wouldn't hurt as much.

"Brad applied to all of the residency programs around here because he knew I was desperate to come home. And I think he was afraid of how far I'd go to get here. He got accepted and started his residency here in June." I held my eye contact with Eliza. She actually seemed surprisingly nonjudgmental.

"He started in June, but you didn't come until October, right?" Eliza asked gently.

"When I asked to move back here to live with Brad, my parents said no. I was their underage daughter and I was to stay with them." I took a deep breath. I had shattered every piece of nice china my parents owned that night; they simply shrugged their shoulders and went back to work. "I started to act out in hopes that they wouldn't want to deal with me anymore. I drank a lot. They told me that drinking was part of the European culture. I lost my virginity to some guy I barely knew in my parents' bed. They brought home birth control from the hospital and told me to use condoms. I tried smoking pot. They told me that marijuana did have medicinal value to it; they bought me a medical textbook on how marijuana affects the body for better or worse. Nothing was working. I was so far in over my head that I didn't even care what these things were costing me. I lost my virginity to a guy who probably doesn't remember my name. I will never get that moment back. Finally, I reached for the last thing I could get my hands on, coke. Do you know I googled how to snort coke before I did it to make sure I was doing it right?" I was now shaking as I was sobbing. "I literally sat at the computer and read about the proper way to snort coke. I was even a crappy drug addict. I was taking my first hit when my parents came home. They weren't alone though; they had brought the head of the hospital and his wife to our house for dinner. That is what sent them over the edge. Not the fact that their daughter was snorting a drug that could kill her, but that she was doing so in front of their esteemed colleague." I stopped for a second as I remembered my dad violently pulling me off the couch and shoving me into another room while they tried to explain away my behavior. Even though I was still looking at Eliza, I could feel Lexie squeezing my hand. "They decided to send me back that night, but there were conditions. First of all, they wouldn't bail me out of any trouble I got in back here. Second, they signed over every single piece of guardianship of me to Brad. Third, they gave me my inheritance and Peter's in one lump sum to 'waste on my drug of choice.' And finally, that I would never contact them again for anything ever. To quote my father, I was to no longer call them my parents because they weren't when the last document was signed."

"That's it," I said, wiping my eyes. "My parents, or Dr. and Dr. Caulfield as they preferred to be called, spoke to Brad at Christmas. They didn't ask or say anything about me. On Christmas day, Brad and I got into a huge fight. We haven't spoken since." I looked down into my lap. "And here I am, back where I started, and nothing is the same. I have no idea who I am anymore, and I don't even know if I made the right decision coming back. Really, I'm going to be the same screw up I am now in any country. And Matt's right. Peter would absolutely hate me for everything I've done in the last two years. I hate me for the things I've done."

"Emerson, you did the best you could," Eliza whispered. "There was no right answer."

"Maybe, but there were a lot of wrong answers though," I replied. "And I have to live with that for the rest of my life. I need to wash my face in the bathroom."

"Do you want me to come?" Lexie asked.

"No, it's okay," I replied and took my first wobbly step out of the room.

Matt

Looking at the locket she left on the table, I knew she took it off because I gave it to her before I knew the truth about her. And to be honest, I didn't know how I felt now. She wasn't the same girl. Pot. Coke. One night stands. Em had certainly lost her girl-next-door image.

"Are you happy, Matt?" Luke asked quietly. "Is this what you wanted?"

"Back off, Luke. Obviously, I'm not happy. I don't even know her anymore," I replied, still sorting through her story.

"You are a self-righteous, asshole." Luke pushed forward and leaned across the table. "It didn't take a goddamn genius to see that she isn't coping well and something happened in France, but you've had her on a goddamn pedestal since the day I met you. You chose to ignore what was blatantly in front of you to hold onto some perfect image of her that no one could live up to. She's a person, Matt. We make dumb mistakes. You've made quite a few this evening."

"When did you start defending her, Luke? Normally, you're the first person to point out how flawed she is." I knew I was reaching at this point. "And after she admits to snorting coke, you just turn the other cheek."

"When my sister came home from shopping with her and made it through a week without crying. Hannah is at a friend's house tonight. Do you know how long it had been since my sister did something with a friend?" Luke shook his head in disgust. "We both know damn well that Em didn't have to take Hannah and that the whole trip probably reminded her of Peter."

I rested my head between my hands because I knew Luke was right. If I looked back at the last few months, there were plenty of times where she seemed disengaged in everything. I knew it then too, but I didn't bring it up because I didn't want to deal with the consequences of what she might say. It seemed easier to ignore it or talk about safe subjects. I was a self-righteous asshole.

"Should I go check on her?" Eliza asked. Somewhere in the midst of the hell that was this New Year's party, Eliza started to care about Emerson. And I was the one who hurt her the most.

"I'll go," Lexie replied, pushing herself away from the table. "Luke was right. None of us can ever tell anyone what she said tonight. She's been through enough." Lexie walked off to search for whatever bathroom Em had holed herself up in.

"I guess we know what they say about smoking pot and doing drugs isn't true," Tyler commented. "I overheard she was high on the list to be valedictorian next year."

"Dude, that's what you got out of this?" Luke asked incredulously. "Seriously?"

"Just trying to lighten the suffocating tension," Tyler replied.

Luke laughed. "You do realize that your dumb ass can't afford to sacrifice any brain cells, right? I mean, she's a genius. She probably could have afforded the few she killed, but you'd be a super senior if you did that shit."

"She gone," Lexie yelled as she walked back into the kitchen.

"What do you mean she's gone?" Tyler asked.

"Unless Luke has some super-secret bathroom in this house that you need to pull out a book to get into, she's not in any of the bathrooms," Lexie replied, looking helpless.

"She didn't take any of the cars," Eliza said, re-entering the room. I hadn't even seen her leave.

Shoving away the mess and fog in my brain, I made a plan. "Lexie, you and Tyler walk over to Em's house. I'll give you the keys and check every room there. Her brother is on night shift so no one will be home. Luke, stay here with Eliza and check all the hiding spots in your house. You know this place better than anyone. And everyone is walking because whatever the hell Tyler put into those drinks was strong."

"Where are you going?" Luke asked.

"Peter's grave. I'm the only person who can find it easily at night. Everyone take your cell phones and send a group message if you find her."

"And if we don't?" Eliza asked as tears streamed down her face.

"Then we call the police and her brother," I replied. I really hoped it didn't come to that, but Em left here emotionally devastated and alone. And I suddenly wasn't sure what she was capable of doing.

The mile run to the cemetery gave me time to think. Em had been through more in two and a half years than I had been in my whole life. And I just shoved her away like everyone else in her family. She trusted me, and I turned on her just like everyone else. The only person who never turned on her was Peter. She had to be at his grave. Even if she was going to leave town, she would go back to see him at least once. I felt certain I would find her there. As I entered the cemetery, I quit running. If she was here and she heard me, she would just take off again. I was the one who had hurt her the most tonight. I walked lightly and slowly through the pitch black toward Peter's grave. It took my eyes a few minutes to adjust to the dark, but when I got within a few yards of the grave, I saw her figure sitting near his headstone sobbing. Before I approached her, I took my phone out and sent a group text to everyone else.

I shrugged off her my jacket and wrapped it gently around her shoulders from behind. She didn't even pick her head up out of her hands. "Please go away, Matt. We've already covered what you think of me." She sobbed into her hands.

"We didn't cover everything," I replied and put my arm around her. Immediately, she tried to tug out of my reach, but I only tightened my grip on her. After a few minutes, she quit fighting against me. "You've changed, Em."

"I look at his tombstone, and I feel guilty of even sitting here. My brother deserved so much more than what I've become. I made that religious girl cry in class? And you know what? I believe there is a God now. If I didn't believe it, it would mean that my brother's life ended two years ago and all that's left of him is a corpse. There has to be something more to this world than that"

"Em, you couldn't have been a better big sister to Peter if you tried. He loved you unconditionally. I was there, remember? And I'm not an expert in theology or anything, but I really do believe you will get to be with Peter again one day. It's his turn to protect you now."

"I've made so many mistakes that I can't take back, Matty," Em cried as she stared at the gravestone. "What if I had noticed he was feeling sick quicker? Before the cancer spread so much? I was his big sister, and he was dying in front of me and I didn't even notice."

"Emerson, you couldn't have possibly known." I held onto her tightly. "Peter wouldn't blame you for what happened. He didn't blame you for what happened. It hit so fast that no one could have seen that coming."

"I was his big sister. I was supposed to protect him." She reached out to trace the letters of his name on the tombstone.

"You still are his big sister. That didn't stop the day he died. You just have to be a different kind of big sister now." I don't know if it was hearing what she went through or being near Peter's grave, but I finally figured out what need to be said. For some reason, when it came to Em, I made better decisions when I thought of what Peter wanted from me. "Instead of protecting him, you have to protect your memories of him, especially the good ones where he was laughing and playing. And instead of letting yourself die with him, you need to live for him."

"I've done a horrible job so far," Em whispered. "You were right. Peter would hate the person I've become."

"You could have killed someone, Emmy, and Peter would have been on your side without asking a single question. He could never hate you. I said those things to hurt you because I was mad at you for never contacting me, but none of what you're going through is about me." I probably should have added that I acted like an oblivious idiot for the past few months, but to be honest, I think she already knew that.

"I can't take back the things I've done."

"No, you can't. No one can. Do you think losing my virginity to Savannah in a closet is my proudest moment? You at least had a purpose for the things you did. How the hell am I supposed to explain dating Savannah?"

She giggled gently in my arms. It was good to feel movement from her that wasn't a sob of pain.

"So I normally don't believe in the New Year's resolution bullshit, but I think you and I should start fresh." I dipped my head to the side to see her.

"Hi, I'm Emerson. My little brother died, and I did a whole lot of awful things to get even with my family. I'm fairly certain that I'm screwed up, and I need professional help. And I can't promise you that I will be exactly like the old me ever again."

"Emerson, I'm Matty. I'm kind of an asshole sometimes and I dated this truly awful girl just so I could say I dated a cheerleader, which may be the definition of shallow. And as of recently, I've been a really shitty best friend." I offered her the locket she taken off at the table.

"I'm not ready, Matty. I need to learn stand on my own again. I hate myself right now. If we're ever going to work, I have to fix me first."

"We need to head back. It's cold out here, and everyone is worried about you." I put my hand out to pull her up. We were quiet on the walk back, but it wasn't the uncomfortable silence that had fallen between us so many days in the fall. It was an honest silence because we both knew who the other person was for the first time.

When we got back into Luke's house, Em immediately

blushed a bright red when everyone stood up. Before she had a chance to say anything, Eliza flung herself into Em's arms. The other four quickly followed.

"If you all keep being so nice to me, I'm going to start crying again," Emmy said in a voice that was heavy with emotion.

"Em, we're all a little screwed up. You were just the only one brave enough to say it," Luke replied as he pulled her into a bear hug.

"We're like the island of misfit toys," Lex added. She took her turn to hug her. "Do you want a girls' slumber party in one room tonight?"

"No, it's okay," Emmy replied. "I know Eliza and Luke want some time alone together. And somehow I have the feeling that Tyler and you both being here was a well-orchestrated plan at matchmaking." Em gave Luke a wink while both Lexie and Tyler looked everywhere but at each other.

"But we don't want to leave you alone with him?" Eliza gestured to me as if I was a thug that just walked in off the streets, which I guess I deserved.

"Thanks," Emmy said, laughing once again. Christ, I could get used to that sound. "But I think we can probably manage to share a bed without killing each other."

We all said our rounds of goodnights, and I swear even Eliza must have hugged Emmy at least four different times. I grabbed our bags and headed to the guest bedroom with Em in tow. While she used the guest bathroom to change, I tossed on a pair of gyms shorts and lay down on the bed. When she came out of the bathroom wearing tiny pajama shorts and a tank top with no makeup, I smiled.

"So Em, are you still on birth control?" I joked and batted my eyelashes at her.

"I don't know," Emmy replied slowly. "Did you ever get checked for STDs after taking a ride on the town bicycle?" As soon as she said it, she clapped her hand to her mouth and her eyes got as big as saucers. "I'm sorry. Why do I keep saying things like that? It's like I have an evil little elf in me that chirps out the meanest things at bad times."

I laughed. I actually thought her comeback was hysterical. "Emerson Kenzi Caulfield, it's not like you were making fun of Mother Teresa. You cracked a joke about a girl who seems to want to make your life a living hell. I think that's fair." I grabbed her arm and tugged her up against my side. "And you don't have an evil little elf living in you. You're really smart and quick on your feet which makes you incredibly good at zings. It's not a change for the worse."

"Are you sure?" Em asked as she crawled under the covers and rested her face only a few inches away from mine.

"Absolutely positive. I kind of like the jokes even when they are headed at me," I answered, climbing under the covers as well. Em crawled to her end of the bed to shut off the light and then crawled back to my side where she curled up. "Goodnight, Emmy." I leaned down and kissed her temple.

Emerson

New Year's Day passed in a flash. Realistically, I knew it was going to take more than drunken confessions for me to get better. With that in mind, I took the second of January off to find a psychiatrist. I knew I was depressed; I just didn't know how to become un-depressed. Apparently, I couldn't just will depression away on my own. When I was little, I used to try to will things to move with my brain. That worked about as well as me waking up and trying not to be depressed. That saying, where there's a will, there's a way, was also, very misleading. Who comes up with those expressions anyway?

I spent my morning researching what kind of therapies there were. They had groups for cancer survivors and their family members, but judging by how well I did in English class talking about cancer, I wasn't a great a team player. There were therapists who tried to help you find God in your life to see His will in action. I couldn't bring myself to do that yet; God and I had quite a few issues to work out in private. There were apparently even hypnotists who could shut off your mind and lead you to your happy place. It would be easier for me to shut off breathing for a minute than it would be for me to shut off my mind. I constantly had thoughts swirling around up there, and how the hell does a hypnotist know where my happy place is? After about two hours of researching, I found a psychiatrist at the hospital Peter died in who specialized in grief and family counseling. I vaguely remember him talking to us about Peter when he was first admitted, but I tuned him out and refused to give up any time with my little brother to talk to him. I had time now. Once I'd called and made an appointment for the end of the week, I moved away to finish my other two tasks for the day.

First, I wrote a note to Brad, which I left on his bed. I told him I still thought he was an asshole for even talking to our parents, but I was in short supply of family members and brothers these days and I needed him. As much as I had missed being an older sister in the last two years, I missed being a younger sister in the last week. Even though I didn't agree with him, it wasn't worth not having him in my life at all. I also told him I was going to start seeing a psychiatrist.

The last task was the hardest. I tried to gather up as much courage as I had on the walk. I stood in front of the house for a solid five minutes trying to work up the energy to say what someone needed to say. When I finally rang the buzzer, Mallory opened it looking as frail as ever.

"Emerson." Mallory stood back so I could walk into the house. "I thought Matt started back to school today. No one is home."

"Matt did start back to school today. I kind of gave myself a personal day, and it's you that I needed to talk to anyway."

"Come sit down." Mallory gave me a worried look. "Are you okay?" She believed I was here because of my own problems; I was already in over my head. She threw off my planned speech.

"Not really," I answered honestly. "I've been screwed up ever since Peter died, and I can't seem to find my way back to normal or even living."

"Em, I'm so sorry. You know you can talk to me any time, right? I won't even tell Matty," she replied, hugging me.

"Mallory, that's the thing. I do need you. If you keep doing what you're doing, I'm going to lose you too. And I'm not sure I'll survive that." I said it all in one breath to get it out quickly. Apparently, I was only brave when I was pissed. Where were Specs and Savannah when you needed them?

"What do you mean?" Mallory asked slowly.

"Mal, I don't want to hurt your feelings." I hugged her this time. "I love you but you are going to kill yourself if you keep starving yourself." I held my breath. I was pretty sure I had just poked a bee's nest with a stick.

"Em, what are you talking about?" Mallory looked horrified.

"You're smaller than me."

"How tall are you?" I asked quietly though I knew the answer.

"Five feet seven inches."

"I am too," I replied standing up. "If you really think I am smaller than you, let's switch clothes."

"I'm never going to fit into your little clothes," she cried.

"Mallory, I will never ask you for another thing in my life if you do this for me." I had already taken my fitted sweater off and was getting ready to strip out of my jeans in the living room. Reluctantly, she stood up and started to do the same. Within two minutes, we exchanged clothes.

Her sweater clung to me as if it was painted on me, and I had to hold my breath in to get her jeans up. There was no zipping or buttoning them. I gently grabbed her hand and pulled her in front of the full-length mirror in the bathroom.

"Mallory, look. I can barely get your jeans over my butt, and my jeans won't even stay up on you without you holding them." I watched carefully as she took in both of us. Her with my clothes draped over my petite frame. And her clothes which I was bulging out of. I waited for her to say something, but she didn't.

"You're the closest thing I have to an older sister, Mallory. Please let your parents check you in to get help for the anorexia. Sign over your rights. I can't lose you, and I don't want Matty to ever have to experience what it was like to lose Peter."

She started to cry, and I wrapped my arms around her. "I don't know when this happened."

"We're all a little screwed up, Mal." I echoed Luke's words to me. "We can both get help though. Please take the help."

"Call my parents now before I change my mind," Mallory whispered.

As soon as I got off the phone with her parents and we switched clothes, we both sat down on the couch and cried. Loss doesn't always come in the form of death. Sometimes it's yourself that you lose, and that may be the worst loss of all.

Matt

"Are you two still fighting?" I asked as I sat on a kitchen stool in Emmy's house.

"She told you about that?" Brad asked.

"She told me everything." I said flatly. On behalf of Emmy, I was pissed at Brad.

"I doubt it," Brad replied, continuing to make his sandwich.

"Pot. Coke. Living here for never contacting your parents again. That's just the SparkNotes version."

"She did tell you everything." Brad seemed a little shocked. "Good for her."

"How the hell can you take your parents' side on this, Brad? Christ, my mother takes better care of our dog." Fully pissed now, I wanted to fight. I wanted to do something for Emmy's sake. And since I probably couldn't find her parents in France, Brad was going to have to do.

"Matt, stay out of it." He didn't even look up or stop what he was doing.

Shit, I was going to fight him. Pushing my stool back, I walked over to where Brad stood and went nose to nose with him. "If I stay out of it, who's going to stay in it with her?"

"Leave," Brad said evenly.

"Make me." I shoved him off balance.

"I can't believe I am considering fighting a high school student." Brad shook his head. "Matt, did you ever think that there's something bigger going on here and I'm not telling you because I don't want you running to my sister."

"Let me be the judge." I wasn't budging.

"Think about it, Matt. Emmy and Peter were already cut off from their will. If I throw my hat in the ring any more than I already have, what do you think will happen?"

"This is about money?" I asked. "Seriously, you are that greedy?"

"I didn't say I wanted the money for me. If my parents cut me out, their already wealthy colleagues get everything. That's a lot of money that could be put to a way better cause."

"You want to get their money to give it to a charity or something?" I asked. Well, there went my fight. Her brother wasn't a jerk at all. He just damn good at playing the game with his parents.

"Basically, something to do with Peter."

"Em would love that. Why aren't you telling her?"

"Because Em is an extremist, and you know it. What our parents did to her and Peter wasn't right. They're not evil, but they really screwed up with Peter and Em. Em looks at all money that comes from them as blood money. Even if it would be put to something worthy, she would still get all worked up about it. So yes, I keep in touch and play good guy with our parents. You know I'm right, Matt." Brad shrugged his shoulders.

Christ, I did know he was right. Em only drove the Mini Coop in hopes of it getting scratched up. She only bought other people stuff with the money she was left. She had a million dollars to her name, and I hadn't seen her buy anything since she had been back. She would flip if she knew Brad wanted money out of their parents even if it was for a good cause. In her eyes, Mr. and Mrs. Caulfield were dead and that book was closed.

Without warning, I heard the front door open. When Em saw us in the kitchen standing together, she pulled the earplugs out of her ears. Bad timing to return from her run.

"Hey, what's going on?" Emmy asked tentatively as she stripped off her UnderArmour jacket.

Glancing at Brad, I answered, "I wanted to thank you for whatever you said that made Mallory check into the hospital for an extended stay this time."

"Oh, well, I'm starting therapy too, so I thought talking to her was at least worth a shot. I'm sorry if I overstepped my bounds by going over there."

"What? No, you probably saved my sister's life today. I tried talking to Mallory about the eating disorder before, and she wouldn't even listen to me. Whatever you said to her worked."

"Well, I'm glad I could save one of our siblings."

"Em," Brad interjected quickly. "A bit harsh."

"Sorry evil elf strikes again." Em gave me a wink. "In all seriousness, I'm glad your sister is getting help. I wouldn't want to ever see something happen to her."

"I know. I also came over to give you a heads up about the English topic tomorrow. The dynamics of sibling relationships." Even I winced when Mrs. Ferguson said the topic aloud to the class.

"Well, I think we can safely assume good old Fergie hates me. That class isn't AP Writing and Composition. It's 'Sit Around in a Hostile Circle and Talk about Your Feelings' time."

"You managed to piss off Ferguson?" Brad asked her. "Ferguson was out to lunch back when I had her."

"You could say we don't get along," Em replied with a shrug.

"Would you just play the freaking game, Emerson? You could have the faculty eating out of your genius little hand if you weren't hostile." Brad tossed a towel at her.

"Oh my God, you are Mr. Spencer from *Catcher in the Rye*! Are you going to start walking around in your ratty old robe and smell like cold medicine?" Em tossed the towel back at him.

"Ah, who was Mr. Spencer again?" I asked. I even read that damn book.

"The old guy at the beginning who tells Holden that he could have tried and that life is basically a game that Holden needs to play better. Start of the book." Em could have probably cited the exact quote and page number. I was the one who was going to have to start kissing ass soon.

"The old guy says that because he cares about Holden," Brad replied with a pointed look at Emmy.

"Holden leaves because he isn't ready to have someone care,"

Em replied.

"Emerson, I'm really proud of you for deciding to see a psychiatrist," Brad said gently. "It's a really good first step."

"It's not weak of me?" Em asked, looking downright fearful of the answer.

"Knowing when you need something is smart. It's not weak at all." Brad walked around the counter and hugged his little sister gently.

"Not to break up the sibling love fest here, but I am probably the one who is most likely to fail English here. Who wants to help me remember who all of the characters are?" Christ, I didn't think asking for help was weak at all.

Emerson

I dreaded going back to school. Sitting in bed, I tried to come up with an ailment to get out of going to school. I mean, my stomach was filled with knots. It could always be food poisoning; I did eat some stale pretzels last night. It probably was better to err on the side of caution. After ten extra minutes lounging in bed, I finally scooted out to get ready. For the first time since I came home, I was going to try not to put up an act. Matty and I called off our faux relationship until I was ready for a real one. At my pace, that'd be about the time that we would both be in retirement homes. Maybe he'd be deaf and not even notice that I was crazy by that point.

Instead of getting dressed up, I tossed on a pair of jeans and my favorite purple long sleeve T-shirt. I put my still wet hair into a side braid, slipped into flats, and grabbed my bag.

I walked to English class. Lex put her arm through mine as we entered the door. I wish I had talked to Lexie more in middle school; she had been a really good friend to me this fall. And even now as we headed into a class where she knew the teacher hated me, she only stuck closer to me. We took our seats, and about a minute later, Matty dropped into his seat. Walter, Specs, and the zealot were already in the room. I was increasingly convinced that they lived there. Except the zealot probably had to leave to go to pray and stuff.

Standing up, Mrs. Ferguson took attendance and started class. "As I told you all yesterday, today I want to talk about the dynamics of sibling relationships. What makes the bond between siblings distinct? I really want to talk through this topic, and I'm interested in how you process the relationships between siblings."

"Well, in *Catcher in the Rye*, Holden loves two of his siblings, and he hates his older brother," Walt said. Good ole' Walt, I could always count on him to say something to piss me off, but I was going exert my right to refrain from discussion.

"I agree with Walter, Mrs. Ferguson. Walter refers to D.B. as a prostitute. He clearly doesn't think highly of him," Specs agreed. I bit my tongue once again.

"Really, Mrs. Ferguson, is the kind of book we should be reading in school?" the zealot asked.

"D.B. is not an actual prostitute. Holden refers to him that way because he went from writing eccentric short stories to meaningless film stuff. Basically, he's calling him a sell-out," I interjected. I really sucked at staying out of things. Put that on the list of things to tell the psychiatrist. "If he truly didn't care about his brother, he wouldn't care what D.B. did with his life. Apathy is far worse than dislike."

"There's still an actual prostitute in the book," the zealot commented.

"Maybe she didn't read that part," Specs chimed in helpfully. "It's easy to lose track of detailed characters if you don't have detailed notes. Can we see your notes?"

"I don't think she needs notes," Lexie whispered under her breath.

"You can see my notes," I responded. I held up my blank notebook and fanned through it. "Sunny is the prostitute that the elevator operator, Maurice, sends to Holden's room. Holden never does anything with her other than talk to her. He seems to be saddened by her job and keeps reiterating that he just wants to talk. Eventually, she leaves saying that Holden shorted her on money. Holden then gets beat up by her pimp, Maurice. I don't really think the book is selling prostitution nor does this topic have anything to do with sibling dynamics."

"We're all God's children," the zealot interrupted

"Seriously, that the direction you want to take this?" I asked. "What about Holden's relationship with Phoebe?"

"Emerson, you are not in charge of the class." Mrs. Ferguson glared at me.

"I'll answer her," Specs replied. "Holden is way too overprotective of his little sister. He's smothering her because he can't get over his younger brother's death."

"He lets her reach for the gold ring on the carousel at the end of the novel," Lexie piped in behind me.

"Which is symbolic of him realizing that he needs to let her grow up." I supported Lexie's argument.

"Yes, but he smothers her because of his brother's death." Specs wasn't letting this one go.

"How can he smother her from boarding schools?" Matt asked. Matt was holding his own in these classes for the most part.

"Holden takes his sibling's death way too hard," Walt decidedly pronounced.

"Seriously?" Matt asked, straining in his chair. I knew Matty long enough to know that Matty would and could easily get into a fight.

"You're just trying to protect your girlfriend's feelings," Specs replied.

And I was passed the pissed off line now. "First off, Matty and I aren't dating, so if you have a problem with me, take it up with me. Second, please enlighten me how one should handle a sibling's death." I took a breath and stared at them. "Really, who wants to go first?"

No one responded. They all just stared.

"Since none of you have the ba – guts to answer me, let me explain it for you. First, you are shocked. You think my younger sibling isn't meant to die before me. And then you feel as if your entire being is being ripped in half because it is. Siblings share a bond that is so strong that it is undefinable. And when your sibling dies, part of you goes too. All you can see, hear, feel is pain. Every once in a while, the pain subsides long enough for you to be angry. Angry that your sibling was ripped away from you. Angry that other people with siblings don't acknowledge how wonderful it is to have a sibling. And angry that you are still stuck here." Everyone around the room was looking at me with wide eyes. "Do I need to elaborate further?"

Specs motioned to Walt that I was crazy.

"Say it." I nodded my head in Spec's direction. "Say it."

Specs finally spoke. "You're worse than Holden." I felt Matty draw in a breath beside me and Lexie gasp from behind me.

"You are a—" Matty started, but I cut him off quickly. I had a feeling I knew where it was going.

"And you think Holden is crazy and ignorant, correct?" I asked.

"Obviously," Walt answered.

"Well, Walter, how does it feel to know that you are going to lose your status as valedictorian to someone who is ignorant and crazy?" I asked.

"You can't possibly know you are going to be valedictorian," Walter replied.

"Mrs. Ferguson, do you want to tell him what my class rank is currently or should I?" I asked her innocently.

"I really think this discussion is over." Mrs. Ferguson sighed dramatically. Unfortunately for her, I wasn't quite ready to drop the discussion just yet. Really, there was not much she could do to stop me anyway.

"I spoke to guidance before Christmas break. You are looking at your current class valedictorian." I smiled as I said it. "And trust me, after the way you've all behaved, there is no chance that I'm going to do anything to give it up."

Next to me, I heard Matty start to laugh. I knew he wanted to beat the crap out of all these people, but beating them up would only make him a stereotypical jock. I planned on taking the one thing away from them that they all really wanted. If they couldn't imagine losing a sibling, I was certain that each of them would feel this loss.

By the time I reached gym class, I had decided that I had in fact the worst kind of schedule: terrible start to my day and terrible end to my day. Once I changed into my shorts and T-shirt, I headed into the gym where I saw a substitute teacher milling around. Maybe she would just make us walk laps all period or something.

"Hello everyone, I'm Mrs. Michaels," the sub immediately began class. "In order to train for the state physical fitness test, I am going to put you into partners. You and your partner must push each other to complete each task to the best of your ability. I have a list with your assignments. Come up to see your partner and grab a stopwatch."

By the time I reached Mrs. Michaels, a decent amount of people were partnered up.

"Savannah Hayward, you are partnered with Emerson Caulfield," Mrs. Michaels called out loudly.

Savannah and I looked at each other and then both began to loudly protest.

"I don't want to hear it, girls," Mrs. Michaels replied. "Partners or detention."

Savannah and I both eyed each other and then she reached out for the stopwatch. "Let's go," Savannah ordered. "Heard you and Matty broke up already. Aren't you any good in bed?" She raised an eyebrow at me.

"It is hard to compete with a closet," I replied innocently. "Actually, wait, no it's not."

"You're a real bitch, you know that?" Savannah lashed out as we walked to the mats to do pushups and sit-ups.

"Takes one to know one," I replied. "You want me to go first?" I gestured to the floor.

"I'll go," she replied. "Pushups first. Don't lose count." As Savannah did her pushups, I dutifully counted out the 20 she did in one minute. Shit. That was going to be hard to beat. Standing up, she grabbed the stopwatch out of my hand and waited. I got into boy pushup position just as she did and started as soon as she said started the clock. I only made it to 18. "Weak," she replied.

I ignored her comment. "I'll do sit ups first since I'm down here. Hold my feet."

"Gross."

"Just do it, Savannah." When she finally sat on my feet, she started the clock. I did 60 sit-ups in 60 seconds. I got up quickly and switched places with her. Kneeling down, I locked her feet into place. Within a minute, she had only completed 50 sit-ups. Looking around the gym though, we were doing drastically better than most pairings. "If you actually want to win the competitions between grades at the end of the week, we should stay partners."

"You're kidding?" Savannah looked horrified.

"Look around, Savannah. If you want to win, I'm your best chance." I gestured to all the other ragged looking pairs around the gym.

"But I hate you," Savannah spelled it out not so kindly for me.

"Get in line," I replied. "Are you in or not?"

"Who else hates you?"

"Does it actually matter?" I asked. When she didn't say anything, I rattled off Walt's name. I still hadn't bothered to learn the names of the other two. "Are you in or not?"

As we walked over to start the half-mile run, Savannah asked, "That dorky kid hates you. Why?"

"Again, is it important? Let's do the half mile. Whoever is faster can set the pace." I stretched my legs.

"I'm not doing the run until you tell me why the dorky kid hates you." Savannah sat on the floor pretending to stretch but really just being a nuisance.

"Fine, he always talks about how the characters in books are crazy for being so upset over the loss of siblings to cancer. Clearly, I disagree. And he really pissed me off today, so I told him that as of now, I'm set to be valedictorian next year. Walt was not pleased." I crossed my arms. "Can we go now?"

Savannah stood up. "At least you didn't beam him with a baseball."

"Taking away the only thing that kid has is worse. He looked like he was going to cry," I replied, setting a quick running pace.

"Holy hell, Emerson, slow down," Savannah said as she struggled to keep up with me.

"You hate me. Use your anger as a motivator," I called over my shoulder. "You'll run faster." From that point to the end of our very quick half-mile run, Savannah kept up with me.

When we finished, she collapsed on the mats. "I don't hate you," Savannah panted.

"So you start rumors about all of your friends attempting suicide?" I asked skeptically.

"I didn't say I liked you. Just that I didn't hate you," Savannah pushed herself into a sitting position. "Look, you came back. I lost my boyfriend practically the second he saw you, so it's not like you're my favorite person in the world."

"I didn't tell Matty to break up with you."

"You didn't have to tell him. He never looked at me the way he looked at you."

"I never slept with Matty." I figured I might as well tell the truth since she was seemingly being honest.

"Really?" Savannah tilted her head. "Do you ever think he'll forgive me?"

"Do I think he'll date you again? No. The comment to Mallory pushed him over the edge," I replied honestly. "Do I think he'll eventually come around to being polite and maybe friends? It's a possibility if you don't push him."

"I still think you're kind of a bitch," Savannah replied with a sigh.

I laughed. "The feeling is mutual."

"Let's go, partner. There's a senior cheerleader who is going to compete at the end of the week. I want to beat her. Unfortunately, you're my best chance." Savannah began to walk to the pull-up bar. "Are you coming or what?"

"Yeah, I am," I replied. Savannah would still probably kill me in my sleep if she got the chance, but at this point, she was preferential to the kids in my English class. And if Eliza ever wanted to go on a public date with Luke, I needed to play a little nicer with Savannah. Sometimes taking one for the team really sucks.

Matt

"Why are they partners again?" I leaned across to ask Eliza.

"Savannah wants to beat the senior cheerleader because she's a bitch to Savannah, and Emerson is the strongest partner she could find in the class. They've been training really hard all week," Eliza replied.

"Someone's a bitch to Savannah?" Luke asked skeptically.

"Even bullies get bullied sometimes," Eliza replied.

"So we're rooting for both of them then?" Lexie asked.

"Yes." Eliza stood up and screamed, "Come on Savannah and Emerson. Go Juniors!"

"Too weird." I leaned back.

"If Em can work with Savannah, you can cheer for both of them," Eliza glowered. For some reason, I wasn't Eliza's favorite person.

I sat back and watched the four pairs of girls stretch on the mats. The guys would have to do this next week. The freshmen looked way out of their league against the much taller and more focused upperclassmen. I looked down at Emmy and Savannah as they stretched; they seemed to be chatting easily. Watching your ex-girlfriend become friends with the girl you are currently in love with just seems wrong. Really, really wrong.

"May I have your attention everyone," Mr. Rudolph spoke into the microphone. "We're kicking off the physical fitness tests with a little competition between the classes. Each class has selected two female volunteers to represent the grade. They will each do every event and their scores and times will be averaged. We're starting with the half-mile run, so ladies please get into position. The first partner will tag the second partner once they complete the allotted amount of laps." Savannah was going first in their two-person relay, which made sense because Emerson could make up time if they needed it.

"Runners, take your marks. Ready, set, go!" Mr. Rudolph blew his whistle.

The gym immediately erupted into each grade cheering on their representatives. From my seat, I watched Emerson cheer for Savannah. Christ, I was in some sort of bizarro world. Even more impressively, Savannah was keeping up with the senior. She couldn't get ahead of her, but she stayed right there with her. The poor freshman girl was immediately left in the dust, and the sophomore girl was about a quarter lap behind the other two. Next to me, I could hear the girls cheering. Savannah and the senior finished at about the same time. Tagging her hand, Emerson started to run. The freshmen girls were completely out of it. The sophomore girl was on the cross-country team, so she was making up time. Emerson and the senior girl battled it out at the front. Savannah cheered for her from the sidelines. This shit was too weird. After her first lap, Em shot out like a lightning bolt. She very easily outran both the sophomore and the senior. When she won the race for their team, Savannah jumped up and hugged her.

"After the first event, the juniors are in first place," Mr Rudolph announced as a junior chant started around me. "The seniors are in second, the sophomores are in third, and the freshmen are in fourth. We will be moving to pushups next."

I didn't know if I had ever even seen Emerson do one pushup in her life. As I looked at the senior she was going against, I realized she might get hammered. The girl was a starter for the basketball team. When Mr. Rudolph once again blew his whistle, the girls immediately started doing pushups. The sophomore runner was struggling while the freshman girl was hanging in there surprisingly well. When I looked at Em and the senior girl, I could tell the senior was doing more pushups but not by that much. Emmy was able to keep it close, and when the whistle blew again, the senior had only done five more pushups than her. All of the partners swapped places, Savannah was going head to head with the cheerleader who made her miserable. When the whistle blew, it looked like Savannah did about a thousand push-ups a day. She flew through them. The senior cheerleader next to her had a nice even tempo but couldn't match Savannah's pace. I had quit watching the freshmen and sophomores. Everyone knew this event always came down to juniors and seniors. When Mr. Rudolph blew the whistle again, he walked over to confer with each class's designated counter.

With a quick nod of his head, he spoke into the microphone. "In last place for this event, we have the sophomores. In third place, we have the freshmen. In second place, we once again have the seniors, which makes the juniors the winner of this event!" Emmy and Savannah clapped hands while the senior cheerleader glared at them.

As they ran through the events, it became clear that Savannah and Em were the most well-balanced team. They took turns being anchors on different events, and when one seemed to be lacking at a skill, the other excelled at it. By the end, it was clear that the juniors had won. Besides the shuttle run, Emerson and Savannah dominated all of the events. Before Mr. Rudolph could even announce the winners, the junior class flooded the floor chanting, "juniors." A bunch of people picked a hugging Savannah and Emerson up off the ground.

When I finally reached Emerson, I pulled her off some idiot's shoulders and hugged her. "Great job, Emmy. I'm really proud of you."

"Thanks, Matty." She gave me a quick squeeze back. "Congratulate Savannah too."

"Are you crazy?" I replied without any thought. "Shit, Em, I didn't mean anything by that."

She started to laugh. "It's okay. I know you didn't mean it, but I would appreciate it if you at least congratulated her. I actually have to make my way out of here, but think about it at least."

As I watched Emmy walk the locker and continually get hugs

from other classmen, I felt so proud of her. When I turned around, I saw Savannah out of the corner of my eye. Of everything Emmy has ever asked me to do for her, this one might very well be the worst. I quickly jogged over to where Savannah was holding court.

"Congrats, Savannah," I whispered as I passed her.

She grabbed my arm. "Matt, wait one second." I let her pull me to a corner where no one would hear us. "She made you come congratulate me, huh?"

"Yes," I replied evenly.

"I'm sorry for what I did to Emerson and your sister." Savannah looked genuinely apologetic.

"Sorry doesn't always make everything okay." I shrugged my shoulders. "Thanks for saying it though." I turned to walk away.

"Matt!" Savannah called. I turned around to face her. "I get now why you love Emerson. And if it wasn't me, I can see why it was her."

I nodded my head in understanding though I didn't really understand any of it at all.

Emerson

"So tell me why you're here," Dr. Mitchell said. He looked to be in his late thirties, and I was suddenly terrified of him.

"I'm Peter Caulfield's older sister," I replied uncertainly. "I'm not sure if you remember him."

"I do."

For a second, I felt better. I was glad people remembered Peter, but then I remembered that Dr. Mitchell had only seen Peter as he was dying. He didn't know the Peter who was full of life. When Dr. Mitchell didn't say anything else, I started to get uncomfortable. I knew I was supposed to start talking, but I didn't know what words to say. How do you collapse two and a half years of slowly dying into a few sentences?

"I'm here because I think a part of me died with Peter," my voiced cracked and tears formed. "I loved my little brother more than anything in the world, and I couldn't protect him. When he was a toddler, I used to check under his bed and in his closet every night. I promised I would never let anything happen to him. And I didn't keep that promise." The tears in my eyes fell freely down my cheeks. It was so much easier when he was little and spooked by a noise in the night or a tree limb banging against the window. I knew how to hold Peter and tell him to go back to sleep and that I would keep him safe. I hadn't kept him safe though; I watched him die in front of me while he comforted me. "It hurts to breathe now. I literally have to convince myself to get out of the bed every morning. Sometimes I hope that I die, so I don't have to continue a life without my brother."

"Have you gotten close to killing yourself?"

"No, I couldn't do it. Peter would hate me for doing it. I have an older brother who already lost one sibling. And I have a few friends who would be sad to see me go. I would never go through with it because I wouldn't ever want them to feel the way I do right now." Each time I had considered it, I had thought of Peter or Brad. Sometimes I had even thought of Matty. Each time, thinking of one of them had stopped me.

"What about your parents?" Dr. Mitchell asked. "Do you worry what they would think or feel?" He was barking up the wrong tree with this line of questions.

"I don't technically have parents," I replied.

"Your parents used to work at this hospital." He looked somewhat concerned.

"Brad is my legal guardian now." I shrugged my shoulders. "The Caulfields would prefer that I don't refer to them as my parents, and I am happy to oblige. It was part of the deal so that I could come back. As of the end of September, I was legally disowned."

"Does this bother you?"

"No, not at all." I answered. "You may have liked my parents. I don't really know. I know they are fantastic doctors, but they were horrible parents. They weren't there for Peter at the end; they dragged me away from the only home I've ever known. As far as I know, the only one of us they even ever enjoyed was Brad." Growing up, my parents did make an effort to go to his science fairs and Quiz Bowl competitions. Dorky, right? They didn't go to many of his baseball games, but they had never showed up at one of my track meets, so Brad got more mileage out of them than I did.

"Why do you think they prefer Brad?"

"He's the child they wanted. He turned out the way they wanted. From the time I was born, Brad was responsible and already looking to colleges. I was the reckless and outgoing sibling. Peter was the kind and quirky sibling. Peter and I didn't quite come in the boxes that they wanted. I think Peter tried sometimes, but they never noticed." For the rest of my life, I would have the sound of Peter crying for his parents imprinted in my mind. His unanswered sobs were some of the worst minutes of my life.

"How do you do in school?" Dr. Mitchell was writing things. I know all psychiatrists do that, but it's a little unnerving to watch someone scribble down observations of you. I wanted to see the notebook. Actually, I really wanted to see the notebook.

"I'm on track to be valedictorian next year," I replied, trying to tilt to see it. "I'm not doing it for them though. The Caulfields would have had me graduate high school at the age of fifteen if they had their way. The AP kids in my English class think that losing a sibling isn't hard. We're reading *Catcher in the Rye* and *My Sister's Keeper*. I'm sure they'll find losing their spot in the top five will make them feel something."

"So you're doing well in school to be vindictive?" he asked, scribbling away.

"Yes and no. I could get As in my classes with very little work anyway. I am rubbing the valedictorian thing in to be vindictive. I'm kind of a bad person sometimes." I rubbed my temples.

"Are you still outgoing?"

"Not in the slightest." I couldn't remember the last time I had actively worked at making a friend. All of the friends I had fell in my lap because of Luke and Matty. I didn't know the names of most of the students in my classes, and I never bothered to listen to them. "It's hard enough for me to get out of bed. To pretend to be happy all of the time would be exhausting." I paused for a second. "Will you be honest with me? How messed up am I?"

"Understandably, you have had a tough few years. Given what you've gone through, I think most people would understand how you got to this point. Honestly, I'm going to need you to do three things for me." Dr. Mitchell waited.

"Go on." I chipped the nail polish off my nails nervously.

"First, I think we need to talk on a weekly basis. You clearly blame Peter's death on yourself, and I can help you move past that without forgetting your little brother. Second, I'd like to start you on a very low dose of an anti-depression drug. Your body has adjusted itself to being in a constant state of pain, and it needs a kick-start to break the cycle. Finally, you need to start doing one thing every day that makes you happy. It doesn't have to be huge stuff. Just little things that you do just for yourself. Can you do these things?" Dr. Mitchell stared at me.

"I need to eventually start to live again, so yes, I will try." I couldn't promise him a happy Emerson in two weeks or two months or even two years, but I could promise to sincerely try to take the steps I needed to in order to get healthy again.

Matt

"Dude, you are going to have to tell her soon," Luke said as he sat down at the lunch table. "You don't even know if she would be okay with this."

I knew that. In fact, I more than knew that. When I started my independent study at the beginning of the year, I didn't know Emerson would be returning. I couldn't back out of doing it now.

"Hey." Eliza scooted in next to Luke and kissed him on the cheek. "What are you all talking about?"

"What an idiot Matt is," Luke replied ever so helpfully. "Savannah's eating with us too?"

I glanced over my shoulder to watch a slightly nervous Savannah approach. When she reached us, she tentatively sat down on one of the benches. "Matt, I heard what you are doing. And I want to help." Shit. If Savannah knew, everyone knew. Luke was right.

"Given your history with Emerson, I'm not sure it's a great idea," I responded.

"Look Matt, that is exactly why I should be helping." Savannah ran a perfectly manicured hand through her perfectly maintained hair. "I was awful to her at first. I know that. My family has a lot of money and access to resources to companies that you need, so do us both a favor and let me help."

"You know she's right, Matt," Eliza seconded Savannah's idea. "Luke told me what you're doing, and if you want to do it right, you'll take her up on the offer."

"Is there anyone at this school who doesn't know?" I asked, shooting a pointed look at Luke.

"Know what?" Em asked as she sat down on the bench next to Savannah. Still too weird.

"Nothing," I mumbled.

"You were clearly talking about something." Emmy paused to

look in my direction.

"Savannah and Matt are dating again," Eliza blurted out quickly. I was going to murder Eliza after this conversation. Savannah's eyes widened, but to her credit, she didn't say anything. Eliza, on the other hand, was just one big barrel of word vomit. "No one wanted to tell you because we weren't sure how you would take it. Sorry, Em. We all should have told you."

Emerson shifted where she was sitting to look between Savannah and me. I had promised to love her forever three months ago, and now, I was supposedly dating my ex-girlfriend. Before I could come up with any other sort of logical explanation, Em responded, "It's okay. You don't have to be weird around me."

That was it? She cared so little for me that she would happily hand over my heart to Savannah without a second thought. I stared at her in awe. I loved her enough that I would wait the rest of my life for her to come to me, and she was just willing to throw me away.

"I think I'm going to find Lex and Tyler. Maybe me eating lunch here today is too weird." Em stood up and grabbed her bags and books. Without a look back, she walked away.

"What the hell, Eliza?" I turned on her quickly.

"No one was saying anything." Eliza gave a tiny shrug. "It was the first thing that popped into my head as a lie, okay? If you had something better, you should have spoken up."

"I'm sorry. I was too busy wondering how the hell Em could just wish me well with Savannah." I was so pissed, but I didn't know who I was pissed with exactly.

"Still sitting here," Savannah chimed in quietly.

"Look, man, maybe this is actually for the best. You need time to finish your project without Em knowing. Eliza, Lex, Tyler, and I will take turns occupying Em's time and keeping her busy. And maybe you should take Savannah's offer to help. If Em thinks you're dating her, it will make sense if she sees you talking to her sometimes." And that is how I agreed to what was probably one of the dumbest ideas of my life; there's nothing like dating an ex-girlfriend to chase away the girl you actually love.

Emerson

"Everyone keeps freaking out when I see Matty with Savannah. It's getting old," I lied. Quite honestly, I hated seeing Savannah and Matty together. My psychiatrist asked me if my feelings toward them as a couple said something about how I felt about Matty. Obviously, it said something about how I feel about Matty, but feeling something and acting on it are two very different things. I had been seeing the therapist for about three months. It was not like I was in the running for the world's happiest person alive, but I had flushed away all the sedatives that I had stashed away in case of emergency. No more possibilities of an easy way out for me. I suppose that was a general improvement. And I did feel a little bit less like a fraud when I visited Peter's grave now, which I still did on a daily basis.

"If you are okay with it, why do you keep bringing it up?" Lexie asked from the passenger seat of my Mini Coop as I drove to Luke's house.

"Sometimes I don't like you," I remarked. "Fine, I care."

"You ever going to tell him that?"

"Not at the moment." I unbuckled my seatbelt. "And you're not going to either." We were picking Luke and Hannah up to go to the park. I wanted to test out my new camera, and Luke, Hannah, and Lexie were my unlucky subjects. I stared up at Luke's house; I suddenly became very much aware that I decided to bare my soul the last time I was here. Before I had a chance to go to the door, Luke and Hannah walked out the front door. Hannah bounded down the steps to me. Without thinking, I opened my arms up to hug her. When I pried her off me, I took a long look at her. My mini-me was thriving; she looked sincerely happy. I hugged her again.

"I missed you, Emerson," Hannah whispered as I hugged her.

"Missed you too, Hannah." I pulled her away from me so we

were nose to nose. "Let's plan to get together more often."

"Do I get a hug too?" Luke asked as he stood behind Hannah.

"Yeah, but only Hannah gets the special ones." I winked at Hannah as I hugged Luke as hard as I could before he was ready for it.

When I let him out of my bear hug, he shoved me gently. "Dork." He and Hannah slid into the backseat and chatted with Lexie as I drove to the park I had picked out to take pictures. Slowly, I had been picking up hobbies that once made me happy. I ran at least twice a week. I had no intention of running compet-itively again, but until it was warm enough that I could swim, running was going to have to do. I also had found a fondness for making mixes of bad pop music and dancing around by myself. Lastly, I had adopted a puppy, Jacks, who was currently licking Hannah's face. Jacks was a golden retriever. I knew he'd grow up to be huge, but right now, he was just big ball of fur that followed me around the house. Between Brad's schedule and mine, we were able to take care of him pretty well. Gratefully, he had been super easy to house train. When my therapist had first suggested that I get back into photography, I had balked at the idea. Too many memories. Dr. Mitchell insisted that someday I would want memories from today as well; though I was still skeptical, I liked the idea of being able to give Hannah a framed photo of her and her brother.

"We're here. Someone put Jacks on his leash," I announced as I pulled into a gravelly parking spot.

"I'll do it," Hannah responded quickly. Before I knew it, she had Jacks out of the car and the two were headed to the park. Luke and Lexie quickly followed. It was at that moment I realized my therapist was right. I did love all three of these people. And the freaking puppy. They could never replace how much I loved Peter, but somewhere in the last six months, my heart had grown enough to let other people back into my life. I smiled as I picked up my camera and followed them.

I immediately started snapping pictures. Hannah ran with Jacks with her hair flying behind her. At one point, she accidentally let go of Jacks' leash, and Luke took off after the poor dog and tackled him. I snapped pictures of that too. I caught the moment where Luke placed the leash in his little sister's hand again, and the three of them rested together in the grass. I shot Lexie as she jumped off the swing when it was at the peak of its height. As they were willing participants, they all dutifully got up on some part of the elaborate playground set. Luke even took Jacks down the slide on his lap with Hannah and Lexie in the lanes next to him.

"Em, you're crying." Lexie walked up to me gently. I hadn't even noticed. I turned and dragged my fingers across my cheeks to wipe away the evidence.

"I'm just really happy, Lex." I hugged her quickly.

"Emerson, can I take some pictures with your camera?" Hannah asked from the bottom of the slide.

"Hannah, I told you the camera was expensive," Luke whispered, not so quietly.

"Yeah, absolutely." Expensive things were meant to be used and even broken sometimes. "Come here, and I'll show you how to work it."

For the next half hour or so, Hannah happily shot photographs of just about everything: Jacks and I having a staring contest, Luke and Lexie arm-wrestling, Lexie and I hugging, me tackling Luke to the ground and then making him give me a piggyback ride. We all dutifully rode the swings for her. Even the now sleeping Jacks was accommodating by staying still in my lap as I rocked him. I had no idea if she actually captured anything with the camera though it seemed to be getting snapped a lot in our direction. It didn't really matter. For those few hours, the world seemed like a pretty okay place to be in again.

Matt

I drove to the hospital impatiently. Today was the first day I was allowed to visit Mallory. Playing by the hospital's rules this time, Mallory was only slowly allowed visitors beginning with my parents. My parents kept telling me that she was doing better, but more than anything, I wanted to see it for my own eyes. What did "better" mean in terms of an eating disorder anyway? From everything I had read on anorexia, and I'd read a lot in the past few years, it was going to be a lifelong battle for her. For the hospital stay, I had bought her flowers and the television series *Once Upon a Time*. Mallory had loved fairytales as a kid; maybe she could still use them as an escape today.

When I finally reached the hospital door and Mallory's room, it occurred to me that I had no idea what to say. Shit. I should have thought of this beforehand. Without a clue as to what I was going to talk to my sister about, I opened the door. Mallory sat up in the bed reading some book. I would be lying if I said she still didn't look fragile, but they didn't have feeding tubes in her anymore because she was willingly eating on her own. Gratefully, it looked like she had put on five pounds. She needed about 15 more pounds, but I figured that wasn't a great opener.

"Hey little brother," Mallory called softly.

"Hey big sister," I responded in the way I had done so many times before. "How are you doing in here?"

"So the staff and our parents didn't lecture you in the fine art of small talk?" Mallory said with a laugh.

"I'm always last to get a debriefing." That part was definitely true. I'm not sure why, but I was always the last person in my family to know anything.

"You're basically just allowed to say you're proud of me and that you're proud of the steps I've taken." Mallory echoed a passive and placating voice.

"I'm proud of you and the step you've taken." I played along. "Seriously, how are you doing?"

"Well, I'm sure my stint in the hospital will make the highlight reel of my life," Mallory answered jokingly. After I didn't say anything for a moment, she continued, "It's good that I'm here. I know that I need help and I need to get better. It's hard being here and monitored all of the time, but I know why they do it. I get why I'm here."

"I really am proud of you, Mal." My voice choked up without my permission. I hated watching my sister sit in a bed looking so fragile and vulnerable. Even though she was older, I had dwarfed her in size for the past four years or so now. Mallory was always the crier in my house. If a sad commercial came on about animal abuse, Mallory had to leave the room. If someone gave her a mean look when she was younger, Mallory would be upset about it for days. When I watched the Grinch as a child and the song came on about his heart being three times too small, I worried that my sister's heart would explode from being three times too big.

"Cole sent me a letter." Mallory twirled a lock of her brown wavy hair around her finger. "He wants to try us again."

I stood shocked for a moment. Even when they were happy, I never liked Cole. He was controlling and condescending. Christ, he used to order meals for Mallory. They took Em and me out to see a movie once, and he ordered a diet soda for Em. Em promptly returned it to the counter and asked for what she really wanted to drink. Even at the age of twelve, Cole told Em that she would be glad one day that someone was watching her weight for her. Mallory had been in the bathroom at the time, but the way he glared at Emmy was terrifying enough that I latched her to my side for the rest of the day. Unfortunately, Mallory had never seen any of Cole's flaws. "Do you want to try dating him?" I asked, even though I was terrified what the answer was going to be.

"I thought about it. We dated for such a long time, and I did love him. Did you know Em hates him?" Mallory braided a strand of her hair so she didn't have to make eye contact.

"Yes, she has always hated him. What about you?"

"It's not that easy, Matty." Mallory unbraided her hair. "I don't want to date him again or see him, but I might always miss the idea of what we could have been. Not everyone finds the love of their life right next door."

"Mallory, 'what could have been' and 'what was' are two very different scenarios when it comes to Cole. And I'm not really banking on Emerson coming around any time soon. It's kind of a one-sided deal when it comes to Em." Over the past few weeks, I had only continued to get annoyed that Em was not at all upset with the idea of me dating Savannah. Emmy still talked to me in class and in passing, but she was spending way more time with Lexie and Luke than she ever did before. Savannah, almost shockingly, had played her part well. We talked enough at school to look like we were dating, but out of school, we only talked if it had something pertaining to the project.

"Em seems interested in what you're up to whenever she comes to see me," Mallory interrupted my thoughts.

"How does she get in to see you?" I asked. Up until this point, only our parents had visitation rights.

"When has there ever been a rule that Em followed if she didn't want to?" Mallory asked and rolled her eyes.

She was right. Em often referred to "rules" as "mere suggestions."

"She comes every week after she has her therapy session. She's doing better, I think. Her eyes don't look so sad anymore. She never asks, but sometimes I tell her what I've heard you've been up to from Mom and Dad. Speaking of which, I go into therapy and you start dating Savannah again?"

"I'm not actually dating Savannah again. It's a cover because I'm working on a project that I don't want Em to know about for the time being." I paused and tried to ask nonchalantly, "Does she seem like she cares that I'm dating Savannah?"

"I don't think she loves it. She chooses her words carefully when she talks about it. And Matty, if you think there is the slightest chance that this surprise project of yours will hurt her, you need to tell her now. None of us are doing her any favors by trying to protect her. She has to get hurt again, so she can prove to herself that she can pick herself up this time."

Emerson

"Can you please hurry up and get ready?" Luke called from the hallway.

"It's hard to get ready when I don't know where I'm going, ass!" I yelled back. "Jeans? Athletic pants? A formal dress? A casual dress? Help me out here." I stared at my closet as I stood inside of it wearing only my underwear and bra.

"Dude, I don't know anything about girls' clothing. Wear whatever the hell a casual dress is!" Luke yelled back.

Reaching into my closet, I grabbed a beige and white striped dress. I tugged it over my head and quickly grabbed a belt with an ornate buckle to cinch the dress at my waist. I braided my hair messily to the side, tossed on some turquoise jewelry, and slipped my feet into flats. Yanking open the door to my room, Luke fell backwards into it. Apparently, he had been leaning on the door. I wasn't sorry. "Will this do?" I asked. "Or do I need to change again because what I'm wearing doesn't have the right vibe to it?"

"That'll work," Luke replied as he stood up. "Ready to go on an adventure?" He offered his arm to me. Sometimes I wanted to hug Luke, and sometimes I just really wanted to kick him hard in the knee. Today was one of the latter days.

"Do I have a choice?" I asked as I eyed my outfit.

"No."

For the first few miles, we drove in silence, and then I started to keep track of how many traffic violations Luke could make within a five-minute period. Once I started to criticize his driving, we bickered the remainder of the car ride. As we traveled, I could feel myself get more anxious. At first, I wasn't sure why. Maybe it was just the surprise. I had never been big on surprises, but as we kept going, I suddenly knew why my body was urging me to run. "Luke, we have to turn around." I clutched the edge of my seat. "I can't do this one yet, Luke. You should have asked."

"We're almost there, Em. Just try to hang on a little bit longer. You need to try to go back though." I felt like I might pass out at any second. We were driving to Peter's favorite fishing spot. I had to get dressed up to drive to a place that would undoubtedly make me cry? I actually considered the risk versus reward of jumping out of Luke's car. If I was lucky, maybe we would crash before we got there which wasn't really all that unrealistic of a possibility. As we pulled down the dirt road that led to the stream and river, I closed my eyes. I didn't want to hear the familiar sounds or smell the familiar scent. Peter was everywhere around here, yet he wouldn't be anywhere when I opened my eyes to look for him.

"We're here, Em. Just stay in the car, and I'll come around to get you," Luke whispered. I still hadn't opened my eyes. I heard his door slam, but I couldn't bring myself to pry my eyes open. I knew I was going to see shadows of Peter everywhere here today, and I still couldn't believe Luke was willing to toss me into the deep end without asking. When I heard my door open, I clung tighter to the seat. I didn't want to get out of the car. Luke was going to have to carry me kicking and screaming before I let go of that freaking seat. "Em, listen to me. I'm going to take your hand and hold it. You need to try getting out and opening your eyes and walking around. If you want to go home at any point, just say the word."

"Word," I replied dryly. Luke pried my one hand loose from his seat. "I can't do this, Luke. Please don't make me."

"Emerson, you need to do this for Peter today." He lifted me out of the car. I scrambled out of his arms to fix my dress when I heard it. I could barely hear the sound of the river and stream moving over the sound of all the people talking.

When I opened my eyes, I was shocked. There had to be a hundred of people gathered around what was normally an isolated fishing spot. Feeling my hand being tugged, I let Luke lead me closer to the water. As we neared the bank and all of the action, I saw the first sign, "The First Annual Peter Caulfield Memorial Fish-A-Thon." Turning to Luke, I asked wildly, "What is all of this?"

"An event to honor your little brother, Em. Let's walk around." As we started to walk, I was bombard with photos of Peter and me hanging all around the area. I walked up to one of the signs, which held an enlarged photo of Peter fishing. I ran my finger over the features in his face. "If you like the pictures, I think I can do you one better."

Luke pulled me to an area where children were getting their faces painted. My little brother had loved to get his face painted. When I took him to the fair when he was six, we'd spent almost an hour waiting while an artist painted the most elaborate dragon I'd ever seen up the side of his arm and face. It had taken me two days to convince him that he had to shower. When we reached the face paint, I immediately noticed the picture of Peter and the aforementioned dragon. Lexie and another boy I didn't recognize from school were there painting kids' faces.

"Lex," I whispered. "What are you doing?"

Lexie stopped painting the little girl's face for a moment and stood up to hug me. "Well, I heard that Peter loved tattoos and face painting, so I enlisted my friend Dominic from art class to help me volunteer to paint children's faces."

"Why are you doing this?" I asked. I wasn't hurt, angry, upset, or happy at the moment. I was on sensory overload and barely capable of forming a sentence.

"Because Peter deserves to be celebrated, and you deserve a chance to remember the good times in his life," Lexie responded gently. "Here, I made you a gift." She shoved a box into my hand. I was aware of Lexie's presence and Luke's arm around me, but all I really saw was the wrapped gift in my hand. Tearing off the wrapping paper gently, I saw a hand-painted picture of my favorite photograph of Peter and me. In the picture, he had just turned seven, and I had my arms around him hugging him from behind so that our faces were smooshed close together. I loved the photo because with our faces so close, I could see the same shade of blue in Peter's eyes as my own. We both had a dimple on just one side of our face. I had almost worn my copy of this photograph out from looking.

"How did you know I loved this one?" I asked with tears in my eyes. I clutched the painting. It was beautiful. "Lexie, I love this. I don't know how to thank you."

"I had a little help picking the photo," Lex replied with a wink. "And as for thanking me, why don't you try to make it around here to see everything? That will be thanks enough."

I nodded my head in response. I allowed Luke to pull me toward the food stand where Eliza and Savannah were working. Instead of an itemized list of foods hanging everywhere, they had pictures of Peter eating his favorite foods hanging on a clothesline in front of them. They had green snow cones and green cotton candy. Somehow, they had even managed to make green popcorn. My brother was obsessed with the color green. Greedily, I stared at the photos. Before today, I thought looking at them was too painful, but I couldn't see enough of Peter today.

"Hey, Em, are you hungry?" Eliza asked with a smile.

"Not quite yet," I replied. "But this looks amazing. Thank you two for doing this." As I spoke, I was aware of people touching my arm in greeting or smiling at me gently.

"Why don't I take you down to the final spot and Luke can help Eliza for a while?" Savannah walked around the side of the table and took my hand gently out of Luke's. I was in too much shock to protest. Luke hugged me quickly and then switched spots with Savannah.

"Savannah, why are you doing this?" I asked as she walked me toward the water. I suddenly pulled her to a stop.

"Does there have to be a reason for everything?" she asked

already looking annoyed.

"Considering our past, yes," I answered. At least with Savannah, I was able to shake some of the fog out of my brain.

"Look, Emerson, I still think you're a brat, but I also think you're a brat who lost her best friend and helped me win a race that really meant nothing to you." Savannah rolled her eyes. "Do we have to have a mushy hugfest and cryfest right now? I don't want you crying over my new shirt. Tear stains are not a good look."

A laugh escaped me before I could stop it. "You're still a bitch."

"Takes one to know one, Emerson," Savannah replied with a small smile. "Come on, I have a drop off designation." She pulled me down toward the edge of the river where Brad, Matty, Tyler, and another guy were helping kids with fishing equipment. "Hell, that guy is hot." Savannah gestured to the last guy.

"Aren't you dating Matty?" I asked as I too appreciated the view. "And that guy is Charlie Evans, Lexie's older brother. He graduated two years ago."

"Seriously?" Savannah squinted. "If he was hot as a senior, he is on fire now."

"Again, aren't you dating Matty?" I repeated my question.

"No, we're not." Matt's voice came from behind me. "Savannah and I have been pretending to date the past few weeks because her family offered to sponsor the event, and she was a lot of help on the decorating side of things."

"On that note, I'm going to go." Savannah gave me a quick hug and scooted back up the bank. "And I call dibs on Charlie. No stealing this one, Em."

"You did all of this?" I asked Matty.

"This project was my independent study. I decided on it before you even came back." Matt stopped suddenly. "Are you mad?"

"No, everything is amazing. Peter would have loved this. There's so much of him here." A tear formed in my eye, and I didn't bother to blink it back this time. "Thank you, Matty."

"This isn't everything. Between all the money we raised today and the donations of some very generous people around town, we have enough money to award a different seven-year-old one five-thousand-dollar scholarship for about the next twenty years or so, and I intend to keep this event alive." Matt paused for a second. "If you want, you can help me pick the winner for the scholarship. I had them submit essays on what they believed it meant to be kind, and their teachers wrote nominations for them."

"I would really love that." I impulsively leaned up and hugged Matty as hard as I could. "I can't believe you did all of this. It's the nicest thing someone has ever done for me or Peter." And it was. I couldn't think of a better way to pay honor to my quirky little side kick of seven years. After being deprived of images of Peter for so long, it felt like I was returning home to all of the the things he loved. It was a really good feeling.

"I'm glad you like it. Luke was genuinely terrified of picking you up this morning because we didn't know how you'd react." Matty wrapped an arm around me.

Suddenly embarrassed, I put my hand to my mouth. "Oh hell, I am going to have to apologize to him. Luke had to pry my fingers off the seat and pick me up out of the car. I may have sworn at him. Not quite sure."

Laughing, Matty looked down at me. "He's a big boy. He can take it."

"So you're not dating Savannah?" I asked quietly.

"No. She did a lot to help out today, but I think she did it more for you than for me. Are you glad I'm not dating Savannah?"

"YES!" I answered quickly, so much for playing coy or hard to get.

"You didn't act like you cared," Matt responded laughing.

"I've had a lot of practice pretending the past few years, Matt." I looked down at our hands that had somehow intertwined without my realizing it. "But I've been driving Lex up a wall about it."

"Good, let's watch some kids fish, and your older brother, the athlete, get tangled in fishing line as he has been doing all morning." Matty pulled me closer to the water's edge.

Eventually, I picked up a fishing rod and tossed a line into the river. I could hear Peter in the rush of the stream. I could see Peter in the smiles on kids' faces as they hooked something. Perhaps most importantly, I could feel Peter all around me. And he was happy and at peace.

Matt

"Why do we have to put on a huge show to ask girls to prom?" I asked. Getting the words "will you go to prom with me" was enough a problem in my mind.

"At least you don't have to do a cheer complete with a cartwheel," Luke replied, lounging in one of the pool chairs at Emmy's house while I worked. In order to ask Eliza to prom, Luke had Savannah teach him a cheer routine that ended with a cartwheel. The best part about it was that Luke was taking the cartwheel really seriously, but he could not straighten out his legs to save his life. It was like watching a turtle turn over awkwardly. "And I blame all those MTV prom shows. Eliza spent twenty minutes telling me about how one guy asked his girlfriend to prom."

"Are you going to help me at all over here?" I was cutting the phrase 'go to prom with me?' out of a huge sheet of foam. As soon as I had it cut, I was going to float it into the pool and light some candles around the area. Cutting foam was not quite as easy as it seemed, and I struggled to punch out the middle of the Os without breaking the rest of the letters.

"It looks like you have everything under control." I had been working my ass off over the past hour, and Luke had been laughing his ass off for the past hour. I really needed to find more helpful friends. Em had helped Tyler take photographs around town to spell out the word prom by taking pictures of architecture that looked like letters. Savannah and Em tried to teach Luke how to do a cartwheel. And I didn't know that Lexie really helped Charlie ask Savannah to prom so much as just give him a gentle nudge, which was all Savannah really needed anyway; she could easily take it from there. "How is Mallory doing?"

"She's getting there," I replied, still frustrated with the foam. "She's put on some weight, and she really likes her therapist.

Mallory told me Em loved the dedication to Peter." I was so relieved when my older sister told me that; I had worried for weeks that I was going to make things worse for her by doing it.

Flipping his feet off the lounge chair, Luke turned to me. "You know Em's getting there too, right?" He glanced at me. "I've heard more honest laughter out of her in the last few weeks than I heard the first three months she was here." Luke took a breath. "She's getting better, Matt."

I let out a frustrated sigh that came both from cutting foam and from feeling like Em was as distant as ever with me. "She's getting better around all of you, Luke. She's still shy or distant or something around me." With a renewed energy, I took out my frustration on the foam. "For some reason, I'm the guy she has to be weird around."

"You can be such a dumbass, Matty." Luke leaned forward. "Did you ever think she's weird around you because you're the one she is trying to get better for? It's okay if the rest of us see her trip as she scrambles up the road to recovery, but she doesn't want you to see her until she's there."

"I would help her if she let me." I held up my masterpiece for a second before gently letting it float in the pool.

"Dude, there are some journeys that you have to take alone." Luke stood up and grabbed his cell phone and keys. "I should get out of here. I doubt Lex and Hannah can distract her much longer. Good luck, man." Luke shook my hand and then walked around the edge of Em's house.

As soon as Luke left, I began setting up the tea light candles that my sister insisted were a "must have" to ask Emmy to prom. Within a half hour, I lit about 20 of those things placing them haphazardly around the pool. Was there really an art to it or was it just like shoving candles into a birthday cake where the basic goal was not to interfere with the writing or icing? It didn't seem like "art" to me. When I finally finished, I paced the perimeter of the pool for about ten minutes before I heard her car pull in the front garage. I quickly sent her a text to come to the back of the house.

"Come on, Jacks," Emmy's voice encouraged. "You're such a good boy. You want to see Matty?" Before I knew it, Jacks, the getting-bigger-by-the-day puppy, was barreling at me with Emmy trailing behind. I was so distracted by Jacks and his overabundance of enthusiasm that I forgot about my whole speech. I had even practiced the goddamn thing. As Em reached the side of the pool, she read the sign I had sent floating an hour before. "Yes!"

Distracted with pulling Jacks off my shoe, I asked, "What?" As soon as I got the words out, I realized what happened. Christ, I was a dumbass sometimes.

"You're asking me to prom, right?" Em asked looking up confused.

"Yes, Emmy, I am asking you to go to the prom with me." I said the words aloud, so they would feel a little more real to me.

"And I am saying yes!" Em happily announced. Jumping over Jacks, she hugged me tightly. "There is no one else that I could even imagine going to prom with, Matty." When she jumped down, she smiled happily at me.

"There's no one else I could even imagine taking," I replied. For a moment, I held onto the hope that Emmy would be willing to risk her heart with me again soon.

Emerson

The theme of the prom was "Dancing through the Years." Corny, right? With Mrs. Ferguson and the seniors as the Prom Committee, I guess I should just be grateful that our theme wasn't siblings who had died of cancer. With our appointed theme in mind, Lex, Eliza, and I all started to get ready for the dance at my house. They boys were getting ready next door at Matty's, which made things convenient. As if my first high school dance wasn't terrifying enough, I planned on asking Matty for the locket back tonight. I was ready to be more than his friend. Over the past few weeks, I had started to make good headway in therapy. I realized now that Peter's death wasn't my fault nor was it my parents' fault unfortunately. Dr. Mitchell said something that resonated with me one day. I'm not sure if he even remember saying it because it was such a sidebar comment. He said that not every person is meant to play every role well. To be fair, I didn't play the part of "daughter" all that well, and "my parents" didn't play their roles that great either. They knew how to be perfect surgeons and perhaps that would be enough for them in life. As time passed, I was increasingly convinced I was meant to be a "sister," "friend," and maybe even "girlfriend." I could be happy if those were the only roles I was meant to fill well.

"Hey Em, do you have bright red lipstick?" Eliza asked as she stuck her head out of my bathroom. Eliza was paying homage to the theme by dressing as a flapper. The showy red dress looked amazing on her, and since she was a great dancer, the fringe was almost always in constant motion.

"Top drawer in the bathroom," I called back. I leaned down and began to lace my light blue heels up my ankle. I had decided to go with a ballet-themed outfit for my dress. My very pale blue dress had tiny straps on it before it dipped into a slight sweetheart neckline. It was very tight on top, and then the bottom flared out to a few inches above my knee. The bottom portion was made of layers of taffeta that swirled when I turned. With my new heels and dress, I looked pretty close to the part of a ballerina minus the whole grace thing. Thankfully, even though I was tall, my bone structure was still delicate enough to pull off this look. For the night, I wore my hair in a high ponytail full of delicate curls. I gave myself a once over in the mirror and decided I was as ready as I would ever be.

"I love the ballerina look," Lex said as she came out of my closet. Lex had gone for the dramatic flair of a tango dancer. She wore a tight black dress that didn't reveal much until you saw how high the slit ran up her leg. Lexie always managed to look stunning without looking as if she had put much thought into it. Lex made her way over to me and held out her hand, and I dutifully twirled with her until we both got a case of the giggles.

"It would be nice if you two weren't so freaking hot," Eliza commented as she stepped out of the bathroom looking nothing short of amazing. "At least I won't have to compete with Savannah till we get to the dance." Savannah and Lexie's brother were taking pictures with a different group of people, but we were all set to meet up there. Just as Eliza finished putting her last earring in, we heard the doorbell ring. I was itching to take pictures with my camera, but Brad insisted I have as normal a prom as possible so he was dutifully going to take the group shots so I would be in them.

"Let's go one at a time, so they each get to appreciate how lucky they are," Lex said mischievously. Lexie never failed to make me laugh. She was as wholesome as could be sometimes, but then she would just lay into someone or come up with a practical joke so good that I wondered just how wholesome little Lexie was.

"I'll go first," I volunteered. Nervously, I gave a dramatic bow and left the room. As I made my way into the marble foyer, I started to wonder if this was such a great idea. Not only were the boys and Brad there, but Matt, Lexie, and Eliza had all brought their moms. That was a lot of people staring at me at once. When I finally entered the room, all of the chatter stopped. Finding myself on the verge of a full on panic attack, I searched the room for Matty. He stood still wearing a tux with a very pale blue tie. I don't think he had ever looked so handsome before in his life. And that was saying something given that Matty's been cute for at least six years now. He smiled as he took in my outfit.

"Em, you look beautiful," Matty announced loudly as he walked over. When he held his hand out, I gratefully took it only to be spun around and dipped suddenly by him. I laughed as my head tilted toward the ground. I could hear cameras snapping around us, but I didn't care. In that moment, all I saw was Matty and how much I loved him.

Matt

How in the hell was I going to survive the night as her friend? Emerson looked like a fairy tale princess who had somehow escaped off the pages of the book and came to life in front of me. In the approximately two hundred pictures we took, I knew I had to be looking at her instead of the camera in the majority of the photographs. I'm sure that wouldn't come off as stalkerish at all. I didn't even look directly into the camera, and my eyes were still adjusting to normal light again. Next to me, Emerson happily continued to snap photos as we walked to the cars. Emerson rarely set up photos; she preferred to take them when people weren't smiling and posed for the camera.

"Who knows where this prom is?" Tyler asked as he opened the door of his car for Lexie. It was good to know that someone in their group still had their wits given that I was likely to just drive around the block for the next hour.

"My dad bought me a GPS for Christmas, so I'll lead," Luke replied, walking down to his car with Eliza. "Matt can follow me, and you can follow Matt." Luke had really hammed up the flapper theme with Eliza. He was wearing black and white shoes and perhaps the "ugliest" hat Eliza has ever seen. She made him take it off for pictures.

Realizing we were at my Jeep, I opened the door for Em. She graciously took my hand and stepped up in. "Hey Matty?" Em asked as we were waiting in the jeep for Luke to set up his GPS. "I'm really glad that it's me and you tonight."

"Me too," I reached over and squeezed her hand before I backed out of the driveway. "It's a little bit ironic that you went for the ballerina theme."

"Why?" From the corner of my eye, I could see Emmy look down at her dress and shoes. "Is this too much?"

"No, you look beautiful, Em," I replied quickly. "You don't

remember, do you?"

"Should I?"

"Your parents tried to put you in ballet class when you were three maybe. After you came home from the first practice, you ripped that tutu off and stomped all over it in your driveway. It might have been the funniest thing I had ever seen. Your parents were mad that you wouldn't do ballet; you were mad that the tutu was 'scratchy' or something. And you had this standoff in the middle of your driveway for a solid twenty minutes." I laughed as I remembered Em standing there in her pigtails screaming about how she didn't want to be a pink little ballerina.

"I was never easy on my parents, huh?"

"You were always traveling down your own path," I commented. "I'm not sure if you ever cared if anyone was on the path with you."

"MATT! BRAKE!" Em suddenly screamed at the top of her lungs. Without even thinking or looking, I slammed on the brakes at the sound of her scream. I looked up just in time to see Luke fly through a stoplight as a truck headed directly for his car. You know that second before something bad happens and you can see it coming but can't stop it? It felt like that second lasted for a year. I knew the truck was going to hit as I sat helplessly in my car. Christ, the sound of crumpling metal the two vehicles made as the truck collided into Luke's car was one of the most gut wrenching sounds I had ever heard. In a daze, I stared at the accident that had just unfolded in front of me. For the second time in my life, I would trade anything for a chance to go back and change history.

Emerson

I didn't think. I just acted. To be fair, one could say I had been doing that my whole life. As soon as Matty stopped the car, I bolted out of it toward Luke's now very mangled car. As I ran, I screamed over my shoulder for someone to call for help. When I reached Eliza's side of the car, I slid down to my knees ignoring all of the shreds of shattered glass. The car had somehow crumpled underneath the truck. I crawled forward enough to see inside. The saying ignorance is bliss? Whoever said it was a genius in my book. I had to bite back the vomit that was quickly filling my throat. I could barely see Luke, and what I saw, looked revolting. The car had essentially caved in on him, and in places, the flesh and metal intermingled too much to tell what was part of Luke and what was part of the car. As I stared in, Eliza let out a strong scream. Refocusing on her, I reached in and grabbed her hand. "Eliza, focus on me, okay? Please look at me," I urged her.

"I can't feel my legs," she screamed suddenly.

"Just breathe and look at me Eliza. That doesn't mean anything right now." I bit my tears for Luke who was clearly dying next to her.

"Holy shit," Matt said from behind me. His eyes filled with tears, but I shook my head fervently at him. He couldn't crack right now. He had to wait for help to come. Behind me, I could hear Tyler on the phone and the sounds of ambulances in the distance. I could also hear Lexie vomiting into the side of the road.

"Why do they look like that?" Eliza asked as her eyes widened in horror. With the tiny bit of mobility the car and her position allowed at her, she turned to look at Luke who still had not made a sound. She screamed again. The sound of her scream ripped through me. I knew the sound. It's the sound you make when you are watching someone you love die unexpectedly.

"Luke?" On the other side of the car, Matty had somehow scooted himself in between the truck and the car. As I went to yell at him to get out of there before everything crumbled, I realized it wouldn't make a difference. A person will grasp at any thread when hope is distant. "Luke, talk to me. He has a pulse!" Matty screamed.

Within minutes, paramedics, firefighters, and police officers pried Matty and me away from the wreckage to get in to do their job. As we waited, I reached up to brush a runaway piece of hair out of my face to discover I was crying the whole time and hadn't even realized it. A paramedic tried to get me to hold still long enough to pry the little pieces of glass out of my knee, but it was as if a part of me was tied to the wreck and I couldn't make myself move away from it. Eventually, the paramedic came to me as I watched them pry off the top of Luke's car. At some point, Matty had come to stand beside me, and I reached down for his hand. I had no idea what to say; I was barely just being there. Though it wasn't much, I hoped my hand was enough.

"We've got the girl on the gurney. We're rushing her to Xavier Hospital," one of the paramedics called.

"Emerson!" Eliza's voice rang out weakly. "Stay with me." Giving Matt's hand a squeeze and hugging Lexie, I climbed into the back of the ambulance with Eliza. As I got a better view of her, I realized that her legs had to be broken to be at the angle they were shifted. I tried not to look down. They had put an oxygen mask on her, but it did little to hide the terror in her eyes. "Luke?" The name came out as a sad warbled cry.

"We don't know, Eliza. All that matters is getting you to the hospital right now." I tried to sound calm and stable, and I held her fragile hand gently. I did know though; I had seen death up close once before. Death took my little brother from me, and I was certain that death had returned for Luke today.

Matt

I paced the hospital waiting room like a caged animal. It had taken the paramedics and firefighters close to an hour to get Luke out of the car, and his heartbeat was weak. I felt a tug on my hand as I paced. Looking down at Emerson, I remembered that we had both changed into scrubs when we got here. Our clothes had a lot of blood on them. Christ, my clothes had Luke's blood all over them.

"Matt, please sit down," Emerson pleaded. "Luke's dad and Hannah are minutes away, and she's only twelve. It's going to scare her to see us like this." Em motioned to the group who was one big mess of torn clothing, dirt, and tears.

"She's right," Savannah whispered. Lexie had called her brother while we were waiting for paramedics to reach Luke. Given how hard she was sobbing, I was surprised that he was able to make out that she was asking him to get to Em and Eliza at the hospital. When we arrived, Charlie and Savannah were already sitting with Emmy. Eliza had been in surgery since the two of them got here. I watched as Savannah did her best to wipe her face and disguise her tears. I let myself be pulled into the chair next to Emmy; I put my face in my hands and bounced my legs nervously.

"I know you love Luke," Em whispered into my ear as she rubbed my back in methodical circles. "But we're doing the only thing we can right now, which is sit here and wait." Without taking my face out of my hands, I nodded my head. "Here they come." I picked my head up to see Hannah and Luke's dad rushing into the waiting area. Luke's dad immediately went in search of a doctor or nurse to get some news, but Hannah came running over to us with tears streaming down her face.

Em took her hand off my back and reached out to Hannah who tossed herself into Em's arms. "Is my brother dead?"

Hannah asked bluntly. Leave it to a twelve-year-old to ask the question we were all thinking, but we were all too afraid to ask.

"Hannah." Em wiped Hannah's tears gently. "The accident was bad, but they haven't told us anything yet. We don't know." Hannah collapsed into Em's lap, and Em rocked her gently as she whispered words about how much Luke loved her and how we were all here for them. As I watched the scene unfold next to me, I realized I had seen Em do it before. In Peter's last days, she would often rock him for hours and whisper how much she loved him and how special he was as he drifted in and out of consciousness.

Seeing Em hold it together reminded me that I needed to hold it together for her. I put my arm around her gently so that she and Hannah rested into my side, and she looked up at me gratefully. I rested my head against hers.

"Are the parents of Eliza Lewis present?" a doctor called out to the room. Christ, I had forgotten they were even in the room. Mr. and Mrs. Lewis stood up and walked on shaky legs to where the doctor stood. Their anxiety was palpable in the air. Savannah stood up but didn't walk over. As I watched the doctors whisper whatever news to her parents, her mother broke down to the floor sobbing. Without further notice, Savannah shot over to Mrs. Lewis, sat down in her beautiful ball gown dress and hugged her. Mr. Lewis kept whispering frantically to the doctor. After several minutes of both Mr. Lewis and Savannah attempting to stand her up, Mrs. Lewis wobbled to her feet. Eliza's parents clutched each other as they began to walk forward with the doctor.

As they walked, Savannah watched them with a very pale face.

"Savannah, is Eliza okay?" Lexie whispered just loud enough to seemingly wake Savannah up again.

"Yes. No. I don't know," Savannah responded. "She's alive, but her legs were crushed in the accident. She can still feel her toes, so they think she'll be able to walk again. She'll have to relearn how when the fractures heal enough."

"So she's okay?" Tyler asked.

"No, she's not." Savannah's voice rose. "She's a gymnast. She's tumbled since I met her when we were five. And suddenly, she might not even be able to walk again. How is that okay, Tyler? Do you want soccer taken away from you?"

"You weren't there," I replied weakly as Emmy cradled Hannah closer to her. "The four of us saw the accident. It was a hell of an accident."

"We don't want to see Eliza hurt," Lexie quickly said. "With what we saw, we're just very relieved she's alive right now."

Mournfully, Hannah wailed loudly into Em's arms. Drying her eyes, Savannah walked over to Hannah and Emmy. "Hannah, look at me. Your brother was a pain in my ass from the moment I met him, but he's also probably one of the strongest fighters I've ever met. He wouldn't die and leave no one to make fun of me." Savannah looked like she truly meant the words, but Savannah wasn't there. She didn't see the shape Luke was in when they finally got to him. I was his goddamn best friend, and I couldn't recognize his face. We weren't waiting for the doctors to tell us about a damn miracle. We were waiting for them to tell us he was gone.

Emerson

My entire life seemed to consist of waiting: waiting to see how long Peter could battle to stay alive, waiting for my parents to release me, waiting to be strong enough to date Matty, and waiting to hear if Luke had done the unimaginable and beat the odds. Here's the thing about waiting. It's like being in a permanent state of paralysis. You often know the light will eventually come, but no one gives you any clues about just how long the tunnel will be. And when in a tunnel with no light, it's very easy to forget that one day the tunnel will end and you will reemerge. Maybe not as the same person. Maybe with some battle scars from clawing around in the dark. But there is an end. As I sat rocking Hannah, it didn't feel like there was an end in sight. We were all trapped in a horrible tunnel where we fumbled around and seemed to be hurting each other.

I was so engrossed in my thoughts that I didn't even see Brad enter the room.

"Emerson, thank God." Brad ran over to me and hugged both Hannah and me in the process. "I'm so sorry. After you guys left, I went to take a nap before my shift here, and I slept through the call. Are you okay?"

"I wasn't in the car," I replied robotically. "They haven't told us anything about Luke, and it has been hours. His dad has been in the back awhile now."

"Let's see what we can find out." He reached down for my hand.

Shaking my head, I mouthed, "I can't leave Hannah." Seeing my problem, Lexie jumped into the conversation.

"Han, I really need a drink. Do you think we can walk to the vending machines or cafeteria to get some drinks?" Lexie asked Hannah gently as both Tyler and Charlie loaded her with cash.

Hannah looked up at me uncertain what to do. "You should

go Hannah. I will find you as soon as we know anything. Okay?" Hannah nodded silently.

"I can use a walk too," Savannah interjected. Her voice stumbled emotionally over the word "walk," and I knew she was still thinking about Eliza. "Can I tag along, Hannah?" Again, the little girl nodded. Climbing out of my lap, Hannah scrambled to grab Lexie and even Savannah's hand.

As soon as they rounded the corner, I stood up. "Let's go." I looked around at the remnants of the group, Matty's head had fallen back into his hands the second Hannah left the room, and Tyler and Charlie looked like hell.

While Brad and I walked back into the hospital personnel section of the hospital, I told him about the crash, Eliza's legs, and how I didn't think it was possible that Luke could make it. I let myself cry as I told him, and he put his arm around me as we walked. We knew what it was like to have a sibling in peril.

When we reached the triage desk, a young nurse immediately smiled at Brad until she noticed me. My friends were fighting for their lives, and this tramp was worried that I was competition for my brother's affection. Disgusting in every sense of the word.

"I need to know the condition of Lucas Andrews," Brad said sternly.

"Who is the girl?" the nurse, Erika with a K, asked. "You know you can't bring other people back here."

"I'm Emerson Caulfield, Brad's little sister," I spoke up angrily. Apparently, despite therapy, anger was still my go to emotion. "I was in the car behind the one in the crash. I rode here in an ambulance with Eliza Lewis."

Erika with a K seemed somewhat mollified that I wasn't a threat to her glaringly large crush on my always oblivious brother. "We brought Mr. Andrews back a while ago to update him on the condition of his son, but he passed out during the middle of it. We have him in room 2b.

Without waiting for further notice, Brad grabbed my hand

and we both rushed to room 2b to follow in the doctors. When we entered the room, both attending doctors immediately turned to us. "Dr. Caulfield, what are you doing in here?"

"Mr. Andrews and his son are close friends of my family," Brad indicated to me. "We wanted to be here for him."

"Dr. Caulfield, you know that we don't disclose this kind of information to friends if family is available," one of the doctors chided him.

"With all due respect, sir, I could have pulled up the file on Mr. Andrews and Luke on my own to read, but I'm doing this the proper way by asking Mr. Andrews' permission to stay in the room," Brad quipped back quickly. I loved my big brother so much in that moment. For all the crap I'd given him, he was nothing like our parents. And he never left me no matter what I did.

"Dr. Caulfield, you will be running labs all night," Doctor One replied. "It will give you time to review patient privacy and confidentiality agreements, which clearly you think you are above in this hospital."

"Please let them stay," Luke's father whispered. "I've known them both for years now."

The doctors eyed us suspiciously, but neither of us a budged an inch. Finally, one of the doctors spoke up. "Mr. Andrews, sir, the car accident that your son was in was one of the worse the paramedics have ever seen. In a lot of cases like these, the driver is killed immediately on impact. There was too much damage to his brain and spinal cord. There's nothing we can do to fix it. We currently have your son on life support in hopes that he can survive long enough for you and your family to say goodbye," the doctor finished gently. Meanwhile, Mr. Andrews' face immediately crumpled, and like his daughter, a wail escaped him.

"How do you know he won't wake back up? Isn't it too soon to know?" Luke's dad was grasping at straws that didn't exist.

"Even if we could manage to keep your son alive for longer, he would never be able to move or think or speak again. Some of your son's organs have already given out; even if we could keep him alive, you would have to watch your son die over maybe a series of hours or days at best." Were all the doctors trained in how to speak without emotion? A father's heart was breaking, and they delivered the news as if they were talking about the weather.

"Brad, could your parents fix my son? If we got them back here, could they give Luke a chance?" Despite wanting to run out of the room and the hospital, I stayed firmly planted. Luke deserved to have people there with him and his family at the end. He had given me a lot in the past year; I could give him my presence.

"Mr. Andrews, I'm so sorry, but no. My mom is a neuro-surgeon, but she specializes in brain tumors and cancer. My father is a cardiologist. Neither of them are really trauma surgeons. I'm very, very sorry." Brad walked over to Luke's father who looked like he aged ten years in one night and awkwardly put his arm around him.

"We normally suggest that each family member and friend take one last time saying goodbye personally, and then you may have whomever you want in the room with you for the end." The doctor was back to business.

"Emerson, can you bring me my daughter? I should be the one to tell her. And you kids should go first saying goodbye. Hannah and I need to be last." Mr. Andrews' voice cracked at the end. His eyes were swollen and red, and he was trying to desperately to hold himself together for his son and daughter.

"I'll be right back," I responded quickly and left the room. As soon as I exited the door, I leaned against the wall for a minute. Luke wasn't coming back.

Walking back to the waiting room, I dreaded having to get Hannah. I knew her father wanted to be with her when she heard the news, but I feared Luke's death was practically written on my face. When I walked into the room, everyone stood up. Hannah was back and looking at me expectantly as she held Matty's hand.

"Hannah, we found your dad back there, and he wants me to bring you to him. Okay?" I reached for her hand quietly. She stared at me with big eyes but accepted my hand. I had to turn away from the group before my emotion broke through as it was threatening to do.

As we walked, Hannah asked, "My brother's dead, right?" No one ever prepares you to answer a question like that. There's no quiz or midterm that asks you how you are going to tell a little girl that her older brother is dead. School teaches you how to deal with the facts and certainties of life; there is no class on the most important things: how to protect a heart and how to heal a broken one.

"Your dad wants to be with you, Hannah," I said uncertainly. "He loves you, and Luke loves you which is why he's holding on long enough for you to say goodbye."

She nodded as tears streamed down her face. When we reached her dad's room, she took off for his arms and they cried together on the bed. Brad pulled me out of the room gently. "I'm going to start bringing your friends back one by one. I'll tell them the news. What order should I bring them back in?"

Without hesitating, I replied, "Savannah, Lexie, Tyler, me, and Matty." Matty should have the final goodbye of the friends. I knew that's what Luke would want.

"Alright, sit here." My brother physically placed me in a chair. "I'll go tell them and bring back Savannah first." He headed back into the waiting area.

One by one, I watched each of my friends enter and head back to the room where Luke was. All of them were crying, and I stood to hug each as they went in and came out. For the first time that night, Tyler broke down in ragged sobs. He worked on pulling himself together while I went to say goodbye.

When I saw Luke's body, I raised my hand to my mouth only to find my hand shaking uncontrollably. They had tried to cover up a lot of the damage, but he was barely recognizable. I sat down next to the bed and touched his arm, which lay unbroken.

"Luke," my voice immediately crumbled. "I am so, so sorry. You're like the twin brother I never wanted but couldn't help love despite my best efforts. You've done so much for me this year, Luke. And I haven't really done anything for you except maybe ruin that New Year's Eve party. I'm sorry about that too. I wish I knew what happened after life, but I have to hope that somewhere you and Peter are hanging out and goofing around. Had he grown up, I think he would have been a lot like you. I love you, Luke. I'm in love with Matty too, but you already knew that. Maybe you always did. I'll do my best to take care of him for you, and I'll treat Hannah as if she is my own little sister. I already love her. I promise to be there for Hannah always like you would have been. You're a hard act to follow as a big brother, but I swear I'll do my best to give her a good big sister. It's maybe the only one job in my life that I never screwed up." I kissed his very swollen cheek. "I love you Luke, always." I stood up and walked out of the room sobbing.

Matt

Waiting to say goodbye to Luke was hell in every sense of the word. I had been so busy trying to protect Mallory and Emerson in the last few months that it never occurred to me that losing Luke was ever a possibility. I watched my friends go in one by one to say goodbye. They all came out with the same broken look on their tear stained faces. If they couldn't say goodbye, what was I supposed to do?

"Matt," Brad's voice rang out. "Are you ready?"

Christ, no. I nodded my head not trusting my voice. When I got into the back, I immediately saw Em sobbing hard as she leaned against a wall. When she saw me enter, she threw herself into my arms. She held me so tightly that I could feel every single sob that tore through her body. "He loves you, Matty," Emerson whispered. "When I was in France, it comforted me to know that you had someone who would stand by you no matter what." I knew she was trying to tell me that I was Luke's best friend, but her words hurt too. I didn't have that anymore. Tugging off Emerson gently, I headed into Luke's room.

When I walked into the room, I didn't look directly at Luke until I made it to the chair next to his bed. I would give anything to be anywhere but there. I took in my friend's mangled body; the guy who always had a joke or a scheme was broken. My friend was broken.

"Luke man, I never thought I would be doing this." I rested my head in my arms on the edge of his bed. "Goddamnit, I shouldn't have let you drive. What am I supposed to do now that you are gone? Who is going to tell me when I'm being a dumbass?" As I spoke, I kept expecting Luke to wake up and smack me on the head, but he didn't. He didn't do anything. "I'm going to miss you, man. Every day."

Brad entered the room with Mr. Andrews and Hannah in tow.

Standing, I hugged them both and gave them time for their final goodbyes to Luke. I couldn't make eye contact with either. I was barely holding my shit together as was.

"Matt, bring everyone back in here in five minutes. I want everyone who loves Luke to be here when…" Mr. Andrews voice cracked with pain.

"I will," I didn't make him finish the sentence. We both knew how it ended.

When I left the room, Brad had already gathered everyone in one room to wait. He held up a crying Emmy. Lexie, Tyler, Savannah, and Charlie wouldn't make eye contact with anyone. I couldn't tell if it was because they didn't know what to say or they were trying to hide their tears. To be honest, I have no idea how long we waited. None of us talked. No one knew what to say. There was nothing to say. In one night, one of our friends lost her ability to walk and my best friend was dying. Luke had held me together the past few years. When I lost Emmy, Luke was the one who forced me to go on with my life. All I could think of was all of the things we were never going to get to do: be seniors, captains on the soccer team, graduate high school, become roommates in college. All of it was gone.

A cute nurse peeked in the room. Finding Brad, she whispered something to him and then exited hastily.

"They're ready." Brad passed the message along weakly. Not looking at anyone in the room, I walked to where Mr. Andrews and Hannah were waiting holding Luke's hand together. Brad and Emmy walked in next; Em had quit crying and hugged Hannah tightly before taking a step back. The rest of the group filled the room.

Mr. Andrews choked out a sob. "I don't think I can do this."

"Dad, Luke wouldn't have wanted this," Hannah cried in response. "Please don't make him stay in pain longer." Once again, a twelve-year-old was the person of reason in the room.

"Shut down the machines," Mr. Andrews ordered and turned

his head. When the doctor turned off all of the machines that were keeping Luke alive, it was as if the room collectively sucked in a breath. Within three minutes and thirty-seven seconds, my best friend was dead. We left the room to give Mr. Andrews time to make arrangements.

"You should all get out of here and get some sleep," Brad told us when we exited the room. "It's three in the morning."

"But Eliza—" Savannah began.

"Eliza won't be allowed visitors who aren't immediate family members for days. She'll need friends in the weeks to come, but there's nothing you can do for her right now." Brad ushered the group to the door. "Em, do you want me try to switch shifts?"

"No, I can go home with Matty," Em answered absent-mindedly as the rest of the group walked out with their heads hung low.

Before I knew what the hell was going on, Brad had me by the arm and pulled me into a corner away from Em. "Can you drive?" Brad asked worriedly.

"Yeah," I replied on automatic.

Shoving me, Brad repeated the question, "Are you okay to drive?"

"What the hell is your problem? I said I could drive." I glared at Brad.

"My problem is I'm about to put my little sister in a car with you behind the wheel, and a zombie may be more alert than you."

"My best friend just died. How do you want me to act?" I went to push past him, but he jerked me back into place.

"Emerson is my Peter, okay Matt? If you can't hold it together and drive home, then don't get behind the wheel of the car with my little sister in the passenger seat. So I'm going to ask you again. Can you drive?" Brad pressed on angrily. "She is my Peter."

Stunned, I had never thought of Brad as this protective of his little sister. I knew he loved her, but I guess I had never given much thought to the dynamics of their relationship. "I'll get Em home," I replied more seriously. "I can drive." Brad backed off and walked over to give Em a hug goodbye. Em clung to Brad for a moment and then released him.

Em walked over to me, and we headed for the car. We drove home in absolute silence. Twenty-four hours ago, my best friend was alive. I had wanted to date Em. I was so cocky that I thought we'd be making out in some room in Tyler's house by this point. I pulled in Em's driveway still deep in my own thoughts. I stopped the car for Em to get out.

"Will you shower and come back over?" Em asked in a small voice.

"What?"

"Get changed and come back. I don't want to be alone right now." Em's voice remained at a whisper.

To be honest, I didn't want to be around one damn person right now, not even Em, but I followed my marching orders. I went home, hugged my parents, showered, and let myself back into Emmy's house. When I walked into her room, Em was just getting out of the shower. She already had a on an old track shirt and pajama shorts.

"Did you want to talk or something?" I asked sitting down on her bed.

Em walked toward me and climbed onto my lap as she wrapped her hands around my neck. Leaning forward, she kissed my neck softly, then tugged on my ear with her teeth, and finally made her way to my mouth where she kissed me with an urgency and passion I rarely felt in any of her previous kisses. Giving in, I wrapped my arms around her and flipped her easily so that she was on her back on the bed, and I positioned myself on top of her. Releasing my neck, she ran her hands down my back as her fingers moved to the tip of my T-shirt. Unless she wanted to have sex immediately, she was going to have to slow down a bit. I grabbed her hands and pinned them above their head as I kissed her mouth and her neck. She struggled against my hands to get her body better adjusted under mine. With Em writhing under me, I was struggling to hold onto any type of control.

"Why are you holding back?" Em moaned from under me.

The sound of her voice reminded me that I wasn't dreaming, and I did have Em willingly reaching for me. And it suddenly didn't feel at all right. "Are you doing this because of Luke?"

"What?" Em scrambled from underneath me to sit up. "You think I'm making out with you because of Luke? Really? What kind of person do you think I am?"

"The kind who is hurting right now and doesn't want to be alone," I responded with brutal honesty.

"And you just happen to be the nearest warm body for me?" Em looked up at me. Without waiting for me to answer, she said, "Go home, Matty." I froze suddenly unsure of everything. How the hell was I supposed to know what Em was thinking? "Matty, I'm serious. I want you to get out of here now."

Without further argument, I got out of her bed and walked out of her bedroom door. We could add this to the growing list of things I didn't understand about tonight.

Emerson

After Matty left, I collapsed onto my bed. I just wanted someone, okay specifically Matty, to acknowledge how much I had changed since I came back. I wanted him to notice that I was stronger than before. I didn't just collapse in the face of tragedy anymore. After he asked if we were just making out because I felt lost because Luke died, it was akin to being splashed with a bucket of cold water. Matty truly believed I would only choose to be with him to fill Luke's void. I already knew a thing or two about voids. You could never feel the void of another person with someone new; it just wasn't possible. No one would ever fill Peter's void. To be honest, it was easier since I had accepted that. When I first came back, I didn't want to get close to anyone out of fear that my memories of Peter would fade. It had taken me four months of weekly therapy to get to that point. Peter was ingrained in me and would be the rest of my life. That part of me would never change. Even if Peter's death had taken a piece of me, it left a piece of him with me. That was the deal with siblings. Siblings always carried a part of their brother or sister with them. I glanced over at the picture of Peter, Brad, and me on the bed stand before I closed my eyes. With a long sigh, I let myself fall into a deep sleep.

When I woke up seven hours later, there was maybe a window of three seconds before I had remembered all of the other events that had conspired over the course of the previous night. Luke was gone. Eliza might be paralyzed. And who knew what was going through Matty's head right now? Without any more hesitation, I went out my back yard to the pool. I stripped off my T-shirt and pajamas so that I was down to my bra and underwear. And I did something I hadn't done in at least three years. Jumping into the pool, I let myself sink to the bottom where I sat and thought.

I remembered one of my last conversations with Peter before he was diagnosed with cancer.

"What happened at school today?" I had asked as I made Peter a peanut butter and jelly sandwich after school. He'd sat on a stool still wearing his green book bag. I had never met a person who loved the color green more in my life.

"We have homework, and I don't know how to do it," Peter replied, looking a little worried. It was unlike him not to know how to do an assignment, and it was even more unlike him to look worried. If he had been anyone else in the world, I might have given him a hard time about his always-sunny disposition.

"Well, what's the assignment?" I asked. I knew then that I would never make fun of Peter's happiness and optimism because I would give anything to take the look of worry off his face.

"We're supposed to write about what we think is the most important day of our lives so far." Peter scrunched up his nose living up to his Peter Rabbit nickname. "I don't know what to write about. What would you do?"

I laughed gently. "That's an easy one. The most important day of my life was the day when you were born. You should know that."

"Really?" Peter asked surprised.

"Obviously, where would I be without my very own Peter Rabbit?" I asked as I reached across the counter to ruffle his sandy blonde hair.

Shaking his head at me, he plucked the sandwich off the plate and jumped down from the stool. "I know what I'm going to write about now," he called as he half-walked and half-jogged to his room.

"What?" I called after him.

"The day my sister told me that the most important day in her life was the day I was born," he had called back loudly even though he was already in his room.

Blowing the air out of my nose, I kicked off the bottom of the pool floor. When I swam to the top of the water, I took a few big gulps of air and let myself sink to the bottom again. This time, a different memory I had long since thought about floated to the front of my memory.

"Want to play chicken?" Luke had asked as he splashed water in my pool at his seven-year-old sister, Hannah.

"What's chicken?" Peter had asked clinging to the side of the pool. At only five, he could swim, but his idea of swimming was a mix of doggy paddling, clinging to the side of the pool, and floating in place. To put it mildly, I wouldn't have thrown Peter in the deep end of the pool despite his insistence he could swim.

"Em will put Hannah on her shoulders, and I will put you on mine. The two of you will try to knock each other off our shoulders while Em and I try to get the other one off balance," Luke responded, swimming toward Peter. In one swift motion, Luke had lifted Peter out of the water and onto his shoulders.

"Get Hannah, Em," Peter begged. I wasn't sure this was the best idea. First, I knew Luke could knock me on my butt easily if he wanted. Second, I didn't know how well Peter could swim if he was the one knocked off by Hannah, but I was a sucker for my little brother. Swimming into the shallowest part of the pool, I scooted down so Hannah could easily climb up onto my shoulders.

"1-2-3 fight!" Luke called. Within a minute or two, I had successfully locked my arms enough with Luke that neither of us were moving much. Hannah and Peter both screeched in laughter on top of our shoulders. Finally, Hannah knocked Peter off Luke's shoulders. My heart thumped desperately as I tried to reach Peter with Hannah still on me. Peter surfaced as quickly as he fell. Apparently, Luke grabbed Peter's hand the second Peter was knocked off Luke's shoulders

Peter had laughed as he held onto Luke's hand for help staying afloat…"

Without warning, I felt myself being pulled up from the water. I opened my eyes to find Matty trying to pull me off the floor of the pool. Instinctively, I fought back, but he had a strong enough hold on me that I rose to the surface with him now choking on water that I accidentally inhaled when he grabbed me.

"What are you doing?" I coughed as soon as we broke the

surface. "You just made me swallow like a gallon of this pool water." Again, I coughed some of the water out of my throat.

"I looked out the window, and you were at the bottom of the pool not moving," Matty replied as he trod water with me.

"So what?" I asked. I was still a little pissed at him from earlier. "How many times in your life have you seen me sit on the bottom of the pool for a while and blow bubbles? I used to do it all the freaking time growing up."

"I thought you were..." Matty's voice broke off, and he started to swim for the side of the pool.

As it dawned on me what he thought I had been doing or trying to do, I swam after him and angrily pulled him back into the pool as he went to climb out. "Say it, coward! Tell me what you thought I was trying to do," I yelled at him. When he didn't respond or look at me, I screamed louder, "Tell me what you thought I was trying to do."

When he finally looked up, I knew I was right about what he was thinking. "I thought you were trying to kill yourself." To his credit, he held my eye contact as he said the words.

This time, I climbed out of the pool, and he didn't try to stop me. "You don't get it, do you? I'm not some damn damsel in distress that needs saving all of the time." I paced the side of the pool. "You treat me like this breakable piece of glass, but if you haven't noticed, I was already broken once. Completely shattered and pulled apart. I did that already once. I'm not that same fragile and scared little girl anymore, and you can't even see it." I stopped pacing and stared at him. "It was exhausting pretending to be the same person I was before Peter's death. I'm not that girl anymore. And that's okay with me, but I can't pretend for someone else's sake. Not even yours, Matt." And there it was. All of the things I should have said to him in the past month and all of the things he should have noticed on his own. It felt good to get the words out. I had needed to get the words out.

"Em, I'm sorry," Matt replied quietly.

"I'm sorry too. I'm sorry I can't be the girl you knew growing up. I'm sorry that I'm not who you want me to be." I paused for a second. "You know what? I'm not sorry for any of that stuff. I can't apologize for who I am. I am sorry that Luke died last night. And I am really sorry that I ever thought I could just return here as if nothing had happened." Without picking up my clothes or looking back, I walked into my room and slammed the door behind me. I threw on the deadbolt as I headed for the shower.

Matt

Walking into my sister's hospital room, I knew I was here this time for me and not her. Luke was gone. After the stuff Em said to me this morning, it was pretty clear that she didn't want me anywhere near her. I was losing people I loved left and right. I didn't know what to do about any of it.

Mallory sat up and smiled brightly when she saw me. "Hey, little brother, I didn't expect to see you this early today. Did you bring pictures of prom?" She didn't know. I almost turned around and walked right back out the door. "Matt, what's wrong?" She asked worriedly and jumped out of her bed to get to my side.

I finally broke down crying. "Luke died last night. Em wants me to stay away from her. Eliza may be permanently paralyzed." I got the words out as my older sister hugged me tightly.

"Calm down," Mallory whispered. "Come tell me everything that happened." She gestured to the two rocking chairs our parents had put in her room. Glancing at Mallory, I could see she was doing well. She didn't look as if a good wind would knock her over anymore. Mallory was getting better, and I was about to throw my crap into her lap.

"I can't, Mallory. Look at you. You look great," I said earnestly. "I'm so proud of you."

As usual, Mallory ignored any compliment thrown her way. "What can't you do?" Even as a kid, she dismissed any compliment with a flick of the wrist.

"Dump all of my problems in your lap," I replied and stood up from the rocking chair. I didn't know where I was going, but I knew I shouldn't stay there.

"Matthew Henry Fitzgerald, sit your ass back down and tell me what happened last night." Mallory gave a tough yank on my arm. It had been approximately five years since anyone called me by my full name. I never told anyone my middle name. The only guy I could think of named Henry beheaded a bunch of wives when they couldn't give him a son even though it was his own goddamned fault.

I sat back down in the chair and started at the beginning. I told her that I thought I was in love with Emmy. I told her what it was like to watch Luke's car and know it was going to crash and then saying goodbye to someone who I'd been friends with for over six years. Finally, I told her how Em kicked me out of her life and didn't look back. I was beginning to wonder if Em had never planned to become attached to anyone again. While I talked, Mallory just sat there and listened. When I finally finished, she slipped out of her rocking chair and hugged me tightly.

"I'm sorry about Luke, Matt," Mallory said calmly. "I know he was a good friend to you the past few years."

"I don't know what I'm supposed to do next. I don't know where to go or what I'm supposed to say. And everything I do try to do seems wrong."

"Where do you think you should be?" Mallory asked as she twirled a piece of her hair.

"I think Luke would want me to be there for Hannah and Eliza. I know he loved his little sister, and I think he loved Eliza. We never really talked about it." I considered Luke's relationship with Eliza. They had been a couple for about eight months. In hindsight, I guess we never really talked about their relationship. We mainly talked about sports, bad jokes, and worse movies.

"Well, if you were Hannah and Eliza, what would you want right now?" Mallory probed. I was starting to think she had picked up some hints from her psychiatrist.

"If I was Hannah, I would want as many memories of Luke as possible. If I lost you, I'd want to know every story there was to know about you." My eyes watered at the thought of losing Mallory.

"I think that's a good idea. You and Luke have a lot in

common and shared a lot in the past few years. I think hanging out with Hannah and telling her about her brother would help her hang onto some memories of him. And you're not going to lose me. Really, I'm doing well enough that they're going to release me in a few weeks and I'll just have outpatient therapy." My parents and Mallory hadn't told me there was an end date in sight. For the first time, I smiled that day. "What about Eliza?"

And the smile disappeared just as quickly. "That one is a little harder. Eliza doesn't exactly like me." At her best, Eliza tolerated my presence. At her worst, Eliza made sure to point out my many flaws. "I think Eliza likes both Savannah and Emmy, and I'm pretty sure she doesn't think I deserve either."

"That's just it, Matt. None of this is about you." Mallory kicked me lightly in the shin. She used to do that at the dinner table when we were kids, and I brought up a topic she didn't want to talk about. "Eliza is going to have to fight like hell to learn how to walk again. It doesn't matter if she hates you. She has a hell of a battle to fight, and she's going to need people there for her. She can call you every name in the book, and it doesn't matter. You need to step up and be there."

Well, Mallory wasn't holding back with me. I wanted honesty, and Mallory was giving it to me brutally. "And Em, what should I do about her?" I asked.

"Here, little brother, is where you're an idiot." Mallory rocked in her chair as she curled her legs under her. "You wouldn't believe Em loved you even if she got it tattooed to her forehead. I am positive that Emerson loves you."

Well, that was not the answer I expected. "If she *loves* me so much, why does she constantly push me away?" I had thought of all of the times I had tried to get close to Em over the past year, and she had built a brick wall between us.

"Because you treat her differently," Mallory said this as if it was the meaning to life. I didn't have a clue what the hell Mallory was talking about.

"I treat her differently because I'm in love with her, and I want to protect her." I felt as if this answer was fairly obvious.

"Does she need protecting? Has she done anything since January that would indicate that she's unstable or having a hard time?" Mallory pushed back.

I thought back over the past couple of months. Em didn't break when she thought Savannah and I were dating. She was better friends with Savannah than I was now. She was the one that stopped our car from plowing into the middle of the truck last night. In fact, she was the first one out of the car and holding Eliza's hand much like she held Hannah for hours as we waited. And I had been oblivious to all of it. I only saw the Em who cried nonstop for her little brother. "No, she hasn't done anything. Actually, she fights much harder now. She stands up for herself and the people she loves." Hell, I admired the way Em took control of English class and managed to find common ground with a girl who once called her little brother a "freak."

Mallory just watched me as I sorted through all of my memories of Em. If I changed the way I looked at just one memory, it was though all of my memories of her shifted. Times when I thought she was collapsing were the same times when she was holding on strong. "Em loves you, Matt. I guess the real question is do you love her enough to let her grow and change?"

Emerson

It had been exactly three weeks and one day since Luke had died. Much like Peter, he was gone, but the ghost of him lingered everywhere. His mom, who had left town over a year ago, returned the day before the funeral. I really wanted to hate her, but she looked completely devastated and heartbroken. Mr. Andrews immediately filed for divorce, but to her credit, Luke's mom rented an apartment only a block away from where Hannah lived and had already nailed down a job. It didn't look as if she was going anywhere. For Hannah's sake, I was thrilled. Her mom may have not been the best parent in the world, but she was trying.

It had also been exactly three weeks and one day since I spoke to Matty. I hadn't stopped loving him in that period of time any more than I stopped missing Luke. I loved Matty, but I also loved myself too. I had worked really hard to get where I was now, and I didn't want to take steps backwards. To be fair, I was sure avoiding him wasn't the most mature way to handle the situation, but I didn't really know what to say. Someone really needed to write a book on how to deal with the important stuff. I could repeat the names of every character in every book I'd ever read off the top of my head, but that was not exactly a life skill that was coming in handy. Maybe someday someone will write a *How to Deal with Emotions and Tough Stuff for the Socially Inept.* I would buy a copy of that and maybe one for Mrs. Ferguson.

A knock at my bedroom door tore me from my reveries. "Can I come in?" Brad called from the other side of the door.

"Yeah, it's open," I yelled back. Brad and I were spending lots of quality time together. I even ate bad hospital food to spend more time with him.

"Are you going to pick up Hannah soon?" Brad asked, rolling around in my desk chair.

"Yeah, I need to leave in like thirty minutes or so." I had been hanging out with Hannah at least two days a week since Luke died. It was the most useful I felt during the week. We went out for dessert before dinner. We played endless games of cards. We talked about Luke all of the time. We went on walks with Jacks. Actually, I had asked Mr. Andrews if I could give her Jacks, but he had a severe dog allergy. I told Hannah we would share custody of Jacks. I just took care of him until she could see him again.

"I need to talk to you about something," Brad said rather seriously.

"Are we having the sex talk?" I joked. "Because you're a little bit too late for that one, and I'm not doing it anyway." I liked to make Brad uncomfortable.

"Gross, Em." Brad tossed a pillow at my head. "Actually, I think I would prefer to have the sex talk. Do you want to do that one? I can get an anatomy book, and we can really get into the science of it."

"What could be so bad that you would want to talk to me about sex?" I was genuinely curious now.

"Our parents. They called and asked about you yesterday." Brad cut to the chase.

"Well, that was lovely of them. It's good to know that they check to see if I'm living once every nine months. Is that it?" My parents, respectfully Mr. and Mrs. Caulfield, were definitely a less pleasant topic. I hadn't made all the much process on the topic of my parents in therapy yet. Apparently, seeing a psychiatrist wasn't like taking medicine. You didn't stop going once you see signs of improvement. You had to keep going to maintain your mental health or at least that seemed to be the case for me.

"I told them the truth. I told them how proud I was of you. I told them that Luke died in a tragic accident, and I was and am amazed by how dedicated you are to helping his little sister grow up." He stopped for a second. "I also told them you were currently valedictorian of your class, and as such, you would be giving a speech at graduation as the junior speaker who says goodbye to the seniors on behalf of the rest of the student body."

That was a lot to absorb at a rapid pace. Still attempting to make light of this subject, I joked, "Well, aren't you like a gossipy old woman?" No one said my joke was any good.

"They wanted to talk to you and maybe come see your speech." Brad rolled a little closer to me in his chair.

"Brad, no. Absolutely not." I wasn't at a loss for words on this one. "I've barely forgiven the cat who scratched my hand when I was seven and left a scar, and you want me to just forgive and forget with our parents. They want to be my parent again because I'm an academic success? Too bad. Screw them." If I didn't hate Walt and Specs so damn much, I would hand over my spot. "I know they're not the reason that Peter got cancer or died, but he was their son. I was their daughter. No. They don't get to pick and choose when they do their parenting. If they come, I won't give the speech." I crossed my arms stubbornly over my chest. A wrecking ball wouldn't budge me on this issue.

"I know. I told them that I didn't think they should come." I instantly relaxed at Brad's words. "We talked for a while. They seemed genuinely remorseful, but I told them remorse wasn't going to fix their past with you. Em, they want to be in your life one way or another again. No matter what you decide, they've already filled your account with tuition money for whatever university you decide to attend."

"I don't want their money." I remained stubborn.

"Emerson, listen to me for one second. I love you. And believe it or not, I don't love our parents because of the way they handled you and Peter. I'm not heartless. The catch is that you only have one set of parents. You hold all the cards here. Let them in as little or as much as you want, but think it over before you do anything." Brad stood up out of his chair. "And use the money for school. Don't be dumb just because you want make a point. You've made your point, Em."

Matt

Taking Mallory's advice, I went to see Eliza even though I knew I wasn't going to be her favorite visitor. I came prepared though: flowers, magazines, a teddy bear. Even Eliza had to like something. At least, I hoped Eliza had to like something. When I knocked on the door and entered, I saw Savannah already sitting next to her bedside.

"Hey, can I come in?" I asked cautiously. Honestly, I felt terrible for Eliza. I might not have known for sure if Luke had loved her, but I knew she had loved him. Her crushed pelvis and legs were a long way from healed. She was in a full body cast from the waist down and would be for months to come. For someone who had spent her entire life doing gymnastics and dancing, she literally had to be in hell right now.

Eliza waved me into the room though, as expected, she didn't look exactly thrilled to see me. She didn't break her conversation with Savannah to talk to me though. "How did cheer tryouts go?"

Savannah uncomfortably shifted in her seat. "They went. I saw a couple decent new girls. For the most part though, the girls who tried out seemed to like the label of cheerleader more than the actual cheering and moving part of things."

"Who was named captain for next year?" Eliza asked.

"I was." Savannah kept clasping and unclasping her hands. "I turned it down and quit the team though." Wow, the Savannah I had known at the start of the year would have killed someone to get the spot of head cheerleader, and she gave it all up. I was impressed.

"Why the hell would you do that?" Eliza screamed angrily. Not the response I was expecting from her. When I looked at Savannah, I realized that it wasn't the response she was expecting either. "Why would you throw everything away? You had everything handed to you on a silver platter, and you just threw it away." The look she was shooting Savannah was one of pure hatred.

"I didn't want to do it without you," Savannah replied hesitantly. "We've done cheer together for the past five years. I just couldn't imagine being on a team without my best friend."

Eliza glared at her. "I don't want your sympathy friendship, Savannah. You haven't been all that great of a friend to me anyway. I had to date Luke behind your back because I knew you would be too big of a bitch to just be happy for me."

Savannah's eyes filled with tears. I didn't know what the hell I was supposed to do or say here. Girl fights were genuinely terrifying. I was hoping to develop the ability to be invisible any second now.

"I want you out of here now, Savannah!" Eliza screamed. "Go!"

Standing up, Savannah left the room in tears. In Savannah's absence, Eliza turned her eyes to me. Shit. "What are you doing here?" she demanded.

It was a damned good question. "I came to see you. If there was anything you needed or wanted." I put the flowers on the windowsill, handed her the magazines and stuffed animal. I really should have planned this conversation more.

"We're not friends, Matt." Eliza replied honestly. "So again, what are you doing here?"

"Look Eliza, I know you and I don't have the best history, and that's probably completely my fault." I paused for a second to try to get my thoughts straight. "Luke was my best friend. And even if we don't get along, we both loved Luke, so I'm here because he can't be."

Almost immediately, Eliza broke into tears. "It's not fair. None of this is fair." Reaching for the tissue box, I handed her tissues as she cried. "Luke should still be here. I should be able to walk. We're only seventeen years old. It shouldn't be like this."

"I agree," I answered honestly. "Eliza, I can't imagine what it would be like to be your position. To have had Em die and be trapped from the waist down. And I'm not sure that there is anything I can say to make any of that better." I reached out and held her hand.

"God, I just called Savannah a bitch." Eliza both laughed and sobbed harder at the same time. "I kicked my best friend out of the room. She is never going to forgive me for that."

"Well, there have been enough times in the past where Savannah deserved to be called a 'bitch.' You just happened to say it at one of the times where I think she was genuinely trying to be nice." I leaned back in my chair. "Savannah will forgive you. She's a better person than I ever gave her credit for, and you are her best friend."

"That's why I never liked you," Eliza said as she wiped away the tears from her eyes.

"What did I do?" I asked genuinely curious. I never really got why Eliza didn't like me.

She shook her head. "You see the bad in people before you see the good more often than not. Savannah was a spoiled bitch. I was her no personality best friend who let Luke use her. Emerson was some broken toy that needed to be fixed. Matt, you don't give people chances to prove to you who they really are."

"I never said any of that, Eliza." I mentally backtracked through all of my previous conversations.

"Sometimes, it's not the words you say, but how you treat people. You might not mean to, but sometimes you only see everyone as good or bad." Eliza took a deep breath. "Luke loved you like a brother, Matt. Maybe part of the reason I never liked you was because I knew Luke loved you, and I had no idea if he actually cared about me or just stuck around because Em made him. And now I will never know."

"I can answer the second part for you. Em didn't make Luke stay with you. To be honest, Luke never took orders very well. There's no way he would date you that long if he didn't actually care about you," I answered. "I know Luke. He wouldn't go through motions if it's not what he wanted."

Eliza nodded her head as she processed what she said. Maybe this was the best gift I could give her: knowledge that Luke cared. "It doesn't matter, I guess. Luke's dead, and I'm trapped here."

"Eliza, it matters. Luke's life mattered, and you were a big part of that. Please don't forget him." I paused for a second thinking about what Luke would want me to do. "Eliza, you're tough. Listen to the doctors. Stay positive. The rest of us will be here for you the whole time. Even me, whether you want me to be or not."

"Thanks, Matt." Eliza clutched the teddy bear tightly.

"I should let you get some rest." I leaned over and hugged Eliza gently. "I'll talk to you soon though, okay?" Turning, I headed toward the door.

"Matt, wait!" Eliza called out to me. I turned around quickly. "I loved Luke. I still love Luke. In the past, I've risked a lot because I loved Luke. And you're right. That matters. The girl you love is still very much alive. Don't let her go, Matt."

Emerson

"Are you nervous?" Hannah asked as she sat on my bed while I got ready to give the speech at graduation. Nervous would be the understatement of the century. I tugged on my sapphire sundress nervously. The dress had two thin straps that crisscrossed at the back and fell just an inch or two short of my knee. "Emerson, the dress looks great," Hannah reassured me. "It looked just as good as the first and second time you tried it on."

"Thanks, Hannah." Hannah had dutifully watched me try on dresses about five times. She had patience. "Why don't you pick out my jewelry for me?"

Like a soldier, Hannah went over to the trenches of my messy jewelry stand and started to look through it. Turning back to the mirror, I pulled my hair into a neat ponytail so that just my long bangs hung free. I didn't want to be swallowing my hair when I gave the speech. "Em, what's this?" She held up a letter I had addressed to my parents.

"I'm going to send that to my parents." It had taken me six tries to write the letter. The first few attempts were viciously mean. I knew it was bad when even I winced as I reread them. By the end, I had settled on honesty. I apologized for my behavior in France, but I thought they should apologize to Peter for not being there when he needed them. I told them I was happy again and had made friends whom I loved. Lastly, I told them that they only had one daughter and I only had one set of parents, and that mattered to me. I hoped it mattered to them. "I don't know if I can ever forgive them, but I don't want to look back one day and wonder if we could have had some type of relationship."

"You hated them?" Hannah asked uncertainly.

"I still don't really love them," I answered honestly. "But I'm also not the best role model in the world, Hannah. I've said a lot of mean stuff and done things I wish I could take back."

"But you're a better person now." Hannah handed me the jewelry she picked out. It was perfect. She had pulled two studded pearl earrings, a thin delicate necklace with pearls woven into it, and three strands of pearl bracelets. The middle strand was pink. Hannah had just made my decision on shoes very easy; I slipped my feet into sapphire flats that had pink stitches and a bow on the top.

"I'm trying to be a better person now." I gave my sidekick a hug. "I promise that I will always be the best person I know how to be for you." I tried only to make promises I could keep these days, and I was certain that I would be there for Hannah no matter what happened in the future.

"I love you, Emerson." Hannah whispered gently with tears in her eyes.

"Hannah, I love you too!" I replied quickly and hugged her again tightly. "I know I'm not Luke, but I have some pretty decent credentials for being a big sister." I didn't want Hannah to think I was trying to replace Luke because I couldn't, but I wanted her to know she was loved very much.

"I miss him," she whispered softly in my ear, and I could sense that she was fighting the urge to cry. "I miss him so much every day."

Forgetting about getting ready and the speech I had to deliver in front of hundreds of people in just a mere hour or so, I bent down on my knees to see Hannah's eyes more directly. "It's okay to miss him, Hannah. In fact, it's healthy to miss him and remember him. I think about Luke every day. Luke loved you so much." I thought about what I would have wanted someone to say to me when Peter died, but that's the thing, there's nothing to be said that makes the hurt go away any quicker.

"Do you still miss Peter?" Hannah asked, pointing to a picture on my nightstand. "Will it ever stop hurting?"

Sincerely considering the question, I plucked at the hem of my dress. "I still miss Peter every day. As for the hurting, it will always be there a little bit because Luke is always going to have a place in your heart. You'll always have him to hold onto even when you are hurting or scared." I glanced up to see if my talk had gotten me anywhere. Hannah was nodding her head, but she still looked far away and shaken.

Whoever decided that I was qualified to give speech was poorly mistaken. What had I gotten myself into?

Matt

When I arrived at graduation with Mallory, the parking lot was slowly filling up. It was Mallory's second day home from the hospital and her first outing. In fact, she demanded I bring her because she wanted to see Em speak. As we got out of the car and walked toward the bleachers of the stadium, I scanned the crowd for anyone I knew or anyone I was avoiding.

"Matt, let's go sit with Brad, Hannah, and Luke's parents." Mallory pointed to the four of them sitting near the center and toward the front. Like a good little boy, I followed my older sister over to where Brad could behead me if he wanted. I didn't exactly get Eliza's anger, but I understood Brad's very well. Em was his little sister, and I had inadvertently hurt her. I would want to behead me too if I were him.

"Hello Matt." Mr. Andrews stood up and shook my hand. It had to hurt him to be at a graduation that would have been Luke's next year. It hurt me to be here, but Em was speaking and Tyler was graduating.

"Hi, Mr. Andrews," I responded quickly and took a seat in front of him with Mallory next to me and Brad behind her. It was always good to know where the guy who wants to beat the crap out of you is sitting.

"Can we sit here?" Savannah asked gently. "I promised Eliza I would record the ceremony for her, and you have great seats." I looked hesitantly at my sister whom Savannah had decimated with just a few words in the fall. Savannah must have noticed my hesitance. "If you don't want me here, I completely understand. Mallory, I should have never said those things to you. I didn't mean them and there is no excuse." Wow, Savannah had grown up over the course of the last nine months.

"It's okay, Savannah. Take a seat," Mallory responded graciously. If I was Mallory, I would have responded with the middle finger, but my sister was better than that.

"Lexie, sit next to me," Hannah called. After Luke had passed away, it had been glaringly obvious that Hannah favored Em and then Lexie. I was only called for bug-killing duty or to make middle school girls jealous of Hannah for being picked up by a junior. She was definitely Luke's little sister.

Everyone chatted as we waited for the ceremony. For the most part, I was completely out of the conversation. I stared at the chair Emmy would occupy in minutes. After graduation, I planned to lay it all on the table. Everyone was right. Without a doubt, I knew Emerson Caulfield was worth both the risk and challenge. She was everything.

When the graduating class started to walk in, everyone stood and cheered. I almost missed Emmy walking onto the stage from the side. As usual, she looked beautiful. She always looked beautiful: pajamas, tear-streaked face, swimsuit, sweats. As I stared at her, she caught my gaze and held it for a moment. Nervously, I smiled at her. She smiled back. In fact, she looked calmer than I felt, and I knew she would be one of the first people to give a speech.

The principal stood at the podium and addressed the crowd. "Parents, faculty, students, graduating class, welcome to commencement." The senior class whooped loudly at the introduction. "As has been the tradition for the past twenty years here, I'd first like to welcome Emerson Kenzi Caulfield, the current valedictorian of the junior class, to say goodbye to the seniors on the behalf of the entire school." We all cheered loudly as Em made her way to the microphone. Tyler even stood up from his seat to cheer for her, which got all of the senior soccer players up and cheering.

"Graduating class, faculty, parents, it's my pleasure to speak to you on this very special day." Looking relaxed, Em continued her speech. "Ever since I came back here to school, a lot of you have compared me to my older brother whom I could never possibly live up to in terms of academia and awards. Some of you have made it very clear to me that I'm not my older brother. Unfortunately, some of those same people failed to realize that the speech I turned in for proofreading purposes was the exact same speech that my older brother gave when he was standing up here doing the exact same thing many a year ago."

"Shit," Brad mumbled. "Did anyone know she was going to do this?"

"She'll be fine," I replied without hesitating.

Em turned so she half-faced the faculty and half-faced the crowd. "At the very least, we all learned something about plagiarism today. And to the graduates, I'm very sorry, but it's not going to be your face that you see up on the screen behind me. If you want to see your fellow graduates, I assume you are all very capable of looking around." The seniors laughed at the joke. "When I sat down to write this speech, I wanted to tell you that all of your paths would lead to a rainbow and pot of gold and every other trite optimistic expression that I could think of at the time. For those of you who will get everything you want in life, congratulations. I'm sincerely happy for you. For the other ninety-nine percent of you, life can be excruciatingly hard. Over the course of your life, you will lose siblings and best friends. And there aren't enough words to describe the pain that that kind of loss causes." I noticed some of the seniors who were closer to Luke dabbing their eyes. They knew whom she was talking about. "You will come up across people who break your heart and people who tell you will fail. And sometimes, you will battle ugly internal demons, the ones who tell you that you are not good enough or life isn't worth the fight. It all sounds very bleak, doesn't it? So why do we it? Why do we press on when the battle seems long and never ending?"

Em had everyone in the place completely silent. Hell, I was starting to wonder the answer to those questions. Behind her the screen lit up. Pictures of Luke filled the stadium. Luke playing soccer. Luke dancing with Eliza. Luke and I at age eight and then again at age sixteen. Luke with his parents. Luke giving Em a piggyback ride. Luke armwrestling Lexie. Luke with his arms around Eliza and Savannah at Peter's memorial. And finally, a series of pictures of Hannah with Luke. Behind me, I could hear Luke's mom crying. In fact, it was hard to find a dry eye in the stadium. Finally, the presentation ended of a picture of Luke handing his sister Jacks' leash, and the two of them staring at each other and smiling.

"We do it for all those who can't. We do it because of all the moments in between those battles. We do it because we find comfort in our families, both the conventional and unconventional kind. We do it because ultimately life is too short, too precious, too beautiful"—Em gestured to the screen behind her—"to not be lived. To the graduating class, I wish you congratulations on the behalf of the entire school, and I also hope that one day you have time enough to stop and appreciate the beauty of a moment. Life truly can be breathtaking. Thank you."

Without even thinking, I jumped to my feet and cheered for her. And then suddenly, Brad and Savannah were standing. Tyler and the senior class rose to their feet. For three minutes straight, the entire stadium cheered for Em's speech and for Luke. She had given Luke the goodbye he deserved.

When the clapping died down and the rest of the speakers gave their speech, I just focused on Em. I went through the motion of clapping when friends' names were called. After what felt like eight hours but was closer to two, the ceremony ended and we were allowed to flood the field.

Savannah nudged me. "Let's go get your girl."

Emerson

After the ceremony was over, Mrs. Ferguson came over to me practically growling. She was my assigned teacher for this speech. Theoretically, I knew I should have told her what I was actually going to talk about, but I was nervous that she would shut it down just to spite me. Right before she reached me, the principal and vice principal intercepted me to thank me for my memorial to Luke and heartfelt speech to the senior class. Looking frazzled, Mrs. Ferguson backed away. I needed to have a few enemies, right?

Given that he was sitting on the field, Tyler was the first to reach me. He picked me up and swung me around much the way Luke had when I first came back to town. "You did good, kid. Luke would have loved every moment of that." Before I could thank him, Lexie attached herself to me. Tyler was going out of state to college next semester, but the two of them were going to try to make it work. Lexie didn't even say anything. She just hugged me tightly while she cried. Eventually, Tyler pried her off me. It didn't really matter. Lexie and I came as a packaged team at this point; in mere hours, she would be back at my side.

"Well bitch, you did it." Savannah stood in front of me with a grin on her face. "Can we just get our awkward hug over with?" Savannah laughed as she hugged me. "Thanks for including me and Eliza. She will love this tape."

"You're welcome, *friend*," I replied with a grin.

"Well shit, we are friends." Savannah sighed. "This is really going to put a dent in my mean girl reputation."

"New year, new enemies?" I asked. The tie that bonded us was our mutual love for standing up for ourselves and those we loved. "We can make a list over the summer."

"Done and done." Savannah smiled. She leaned in to whisper, "You look hot. Don't blow it with Matt."

Before I could even respond to her, I was assaulted by Hannah who hugged me with everything she had. "It was perfect, Em." Hannah was still crying, but I hoped they were happy tears.

From behind her, her parents appeared, Mr. Andrews spoke for both. Luke's mom was still crying. "Emerson, we wanted to thank you for what you've done for our daughter and what you did for our son today. It helps us to know that he isn't forgotten. Maybe you could give us a copy of the presentation. I'm not sure we have all of those pictures."

"I will, sir. And your son, Luke, will never be forgotten." I leaned down and gave Hannah a final squeeze. "And you Hannah, I will see in two days, okay?" I felt her nod against me before she went back to her parents.

I grimaced when I saw Brad walking toward me. He wasn't necessarily fond of my methods. He hugged me quickly when he reached me. Still no words. Not good at all. "Just say it, Brad. I'm an idiot. I shouldn't have pulled a stunt like that."

He laughed. "I'm more annoyed that your speech was better than mine. What you did for Luke and his family was the right thing to do. You ready to go home?" Brad had driven me here and was, in fact, my ride.

Looking behind him, I noticed Mallory and Matt. "Actually, can you give Mal a ride home so I can talk to Matt?" I gave my older brother my best puppy-dog face.

Shaking his head, he glanced at Mallory. "Mallory, you're coming home with me. The young kids are sending our old butts home." Mallory started to laugh and gave me a quick hug before heading out to the cars leaving only Matt in front of me.

"Walk?" Matty asked and put out his hand. Without hesitating, I put my hand in his where it was meant to be. We walked to the deserted soccer field in silence. When we arrived, I saw Luke scoring goals and Peter trying to bounce a ball off his knee like Matty.

Pulling my hand away from him, I yelled, "There's something

I have to do." In rapid succession, I did two cartwheels. One for Luke and his inability ever to do a cartwheel. And one for Eliza who might not have the chance again.

Matty laughed as he watched me. "You know I just saw your underwear, right?"

Smiling, I walked back to him. "You saw more than that on the day of the pool incident." He started to say something but I clapped my hand over his mouth. "I need to go first, okay? I love you, Matthew Fitzgerald. You're my home. And I know I'm difficult. I'm stubborn. I say things I shouldn't. And I don't like to let people get close to me, but I can't lose you." I took my hand away from his mouth. "You may talk now."

He smiled and pulled me down so we tumbled into the grass together. "I love you too, Emerson Caulfield. I love that you're feisty. I love that you stand up for yourself and what you believe in, and I want nothing more than to be your home." He pulled out the necklace he gave me at Christmas. I nodded my head this time. "It comes with a second gift this time." He pulled out a charm bracelet that had a few charms on it. Stunned, I studied it closer. "A lion because you're the most courageous person I know." He moved his finger to the next charm. "A charm that says 'big sister' because I can't think of anyone who is better at it than you." He moved onto the next one. "Peter's birthstone and Luke's birthstone because you will never forget them." My eyes filled with tears. "A heart because let's face it, you've had mine since the day you were born." He snapped it on my wrist gently. "I'm not great with emotions, Emmy. You'll probably have to tell me exactly how you feel every day, but I do see you clearly now. And I'm more in love with you than ever."

Reaching up, I gently pulled him down to my face to kiss him. I was lying in the middle of the soccer field in a nice dress in the grass making out. It was one of the best moments of my life. As he kissed me, I could feel his smile, which made me smile in return. "You're wrong, you know?" I got out between kisses to his lips.

"Mmmm, about what?" Matt didn't bother to stop kissing me to talk. I loved this boy.

"I think my best role to date may be your girlfriend." I stopped kissing him, but pulled him in closer. "I've been vying for this position for a while now."

"You were always a lock." Matt delivered a series of kisses to my neck that made me giggle.

Hours later, the two of us were still lying in the soccer field. I forgot about time when Matty kissed me. It wasn't the worst thing in the world. "What are you thinking about?" He kissed my forehead after he asked.

"Where we're going to apply to colleges," I answered honestly. I had been thinking about that stuff recently. "I think we should apply to all of the same schools or at least schools in the same city."

"Em, you could get into any school you wanted. I don't want to hold you back." He brushed the bangs out of my face as he leaned over me. "You deserve the best."

"I know which is why I want you near me." Leaning up, I kissed the tip of his nose. "We've been through a lot of hard stuff the past three years. I want my happily ever after. And there's no version of happily ever after for me that doesn't include you." I looked up at him sincerely.

He leaned down and kissed me hard against the mouth. I let my hands roam freely. Pulling apart for a second, I laughed. "I'll take that as a yes?"

"Yes to everything." Matty pulled me into another long kiss.

I found my beautiful moment, and for the time being, the world was a pretty spectacular place.

Book Club Discussion Questions

1. Is it harder to change or watch someone you love change? Which character changed the most over the course of the novel?
2. Which character did you find the most sympathetic? Why?
3. One of the cornerstones of this book is the relationship between siblings. Which siblings do you think had the healthiest relationship? Explain your choice.
4. If you could have dinner with one character, which character would you pick and why?
5. Imagine the book from the point of view of Emerson and Brad's parents. How might that change the story?
6. Which revelation shocked you the most? Looking at it in hindsight, were there clues that built up to that specific revelation? What did it tell you about the character?
7. Does the first book leave you with any questions? Post them to twitter and Goodreads, and I will do my best to answer them!

Acknowledgments

I have been given the world's greatest set of parents. No matter what I have faced, you have always stood beside me. Honestly, I wouldn't have the confidence or the compassion to even attempt writing if it wasn't for you. You taught me the value of work ethic and the pride that comes along with it. Mom and Dad, I couldn't love you any more if I possibly tried, and even I don't have enough words to tell you how much your support and encouragement has meant to me. I would need a whole separate book to write that story. Every good part of me comes from one of you. I don't know who I would be without the two of you. Thanking you for spending the last 28 years of your lives going through every emotion with me, and we all know there were some years where I had one too many emotions.

To my older brother, Craig, you set the bar high for me in life. Since we both know there's nothing I love more than a competition, you inadvertently forced me to do better than I thought I was capable of doing. You've also shoved me out of my pity parties when I needed to be shoved and defended me when I needed it. In addition to being a wonderful older brother, you married the woman who kept me writing. Jen, I probably would have stopped after ten pages if you hadn't continued to ask me if there was more to read and continually given me positive feedback. You're the best kind of reader because your excitement alone can push any writer out of her writer's block. Plus, you both gave me the world's best gift: nephews. I can't imagine a world without Brady and Carson in it.

To all of my friends and family, you support me no matter how crazy my idea is or how much I've made a mess of things. Kate, Kelly, and Elena, how can I possibly thank you for over a decade of friendship? When I look at my life, I can't help but be grateful that I have so many people who would do so much for me. I love you all. I truly believe my fate in life was to be surrounded by brilliant women for friends and protective men for family. Mukai and Bethany, thank you for acting as test readers for me since my junior year of college. If you know me, you know that I very begrudgingly let other people read my writing when it's a draft. I trust you two completely.

Julie, I think it's safe to say neither of us would have ever guessed you would one day be standing in my parents' kitchen helping me bake cookies for my wedding. We both know you will always hold a special place in my heart.

To all students past and present, you have taught me so much. Every day, I am left completely amazed by your strength, your intelligence, and your compassion. You made me want to write because you are so much more complicated than the way teenagers are stereotyped. I am absolutely grateful that I had the chance to teach all of you. You ultimately changed me for the better whether I realized it at the time or not. I'm pretty confident in your generation. Go out and kick butt.

To the reader, I started writing because I love reading so much. There is nothing I love more than falling into a good book and slipping into lives of other characters. Thank you for sharing the same passion. I always love to hear from you. Find me on Goodreads or Twitter!

To everyone at Lodestone and John Hunt Publishing, especially Maria Moloney, thank you for taking a chance on an unknown. I want to thank you all so much for the support and work you put into this book. I also need to thank Trevor Greenfield who has every right to want to kill me for all of the questions I sent his way during this process. Trevor, you're a saint.

Last but not least, Zachary. We may have taken the scenic route, but it has always been you. I love you. Happy first year of marriage! Zach, thank you for caring about my dreams even when I wanted to give up on them. It's easy to care about your own dreams; it's much harder to care about someone else's dreams. You remind me every day what it is that I want, and your support means everything to me.

About the Author

Instead of doing this the traditional way, I let the people who know me best ask me questions. I think it is more interesting than my resume. For those who want to know, I attended the University of Pittsburgh for both my B.A. in Literature and my M.A.T in Education.

Question from Craig (my older brother): What are your hobbies?
Napping and eating. Those are seriously my first two answers. I also love to read. My guilty pleasure is definitely television; MTV may no longer play music videos, but I fully admit as a 28-year-old that I am addicted to some of those shows. I love cuddling with my dogs, Belle and Bailey. I love spending time with family, especially my nephews. I will play any and all board games. I'm definitely more of a summer person. I like to swim and golf. I like baseball games because it's the only sport where you randomly get to sing a song during the middle of the game. Go Bucs! On that note, I am also a big supporter of bad singing and dancing.

Question from Zach (my husband): What is the most surprising thing about you?
I have a ton of really odd quirks. I determine if it's going to be a good day or a bad day by whatever song is on the radio. When I walk out of a building, I like to pretend it's exploding behind me despite the fact that I can't light a match or a lighter for that matter. I chalk that one up to being a huge fan of the television show, 24. I can inexplicably do wall sits and sit-ups for longer than anyone I know. A shark swam within six feet of me in the ocean once, and it wasn't one of those swimming with sharks encounters where I had a cage between me and the shark.

Question from Craig: Do you share any characteristics of the characters?

I do. I would say I share Emerson's competitiveness and sense of sarcasm. Her voice is closest to my own. I relate to Mallory and her fear of not being good enough. I have Matt's loyalty. With that said, I am like Savannah when I feel betrayed. I definitely have her temper and occasionally her lack of filter. Like Luke, I am an instigator in the best possible way. I think I have Lexie's compassion and open-mindedness. Out of all of the characters, I am least like Eliza and Tyler.

Question from my Mom: What does family mean to you?

Everything. While Emerson's voice is closest to mine, her life is very different. I have two amazing parents and one hell of an older brother. Truly, I am so lucky in the family department. I have two funny and adorable nephews whom I couldn't love more if I tried. Last year, I got married to a truly supportive and incredible guy. Honestly, family is my first priority.

Question from my Mom and Jen (sister-in-law): What inspires your writing?

Initially, I started to write as a way to procrastinate on wedding planning. I did not get the bridezilla gene. What better excuse than "I'm writing a book"? I've always had a bunch of ideas always swirling around in my head. When I sat down to write this book, I wanted to present a strong female heroine and that can be difficult to find out of the fantasy realm. I've also always been interested in the dynamics between siblings. Growing up, friends and family would tell me that I was an only child since there is close to a nine-year age difference between my brother and me. My response to those statements was always the same. "I have an older brother, particularly that guy standing over there." Despite the age difference, I am really close to my brother. Standing back, it's interesting to me how that bond formed and changed over time.

Question from my Dad: What is the most embarrassing thing you have done?

We were talking about immigration in AP American History. I had just transferred high schools, and we had done an entire unit on immigration the year at my first high school. The man who taught AP American History was terrifying, and I mean that in the best way possible. As a teacher now, I recognize a little fear goes a long way. After class, I stayed to give him this really great immigration website we had used last year. He wrote it on the board for his following classes. When I walked into school the next day, all of these guys that I barely knew were high fiving me and patting me on the back for such a good prank. Apparently, I had misspelled the website, and that one letter made the difference between an immigration website and a porn website. I can still hear that teacher bellow "Coleman" down the hallway at me. I quit trying to suck up after that day.

Question Jen would have asked but deemed inappropriate: Who is in your top five?

For the record, my sister-in-law has the best top five I've ever heard, but I won't share it because I don't think she would be amused. John Krasinski. I am a huge fan of The Office, and have you seen his lip sync battle with Jimmy Fallon? Nothing short of amazing. Adam Levine. He is the sexiest man alive according to People magazine. Who am I to disagree? Ian Somerhalder. I refuse to watch the episode of Lost where Boone dies, and the guy has beautiful eyes and does a ton of charity work. Dylan O'Brien. I am positive he is younger than I am, so let's not focus on the math there. He does comedy well, and he has the longest eyelashes. If you can't tell, I like guys with a sense of humor and nice eyes. Finally, Jesse Williams. I love Cabin in the Woods and Grey's Anatomy.

Question from Zach: What is the most courageous thing you have ever done?

When he first asked me this question, I froze, but the answer was in front of me the whole time. The most courageous thing I've ever done is releasing this book. Whether I meant to or not, pieces of me slipped through the cracks and into the writing in various places. Both the book and I will be judged, and I'm doing it anyway. While I'm not any one character in the book, there are fragments of me in each of them. Though I haven't lost a sibling, I have battled depression. It was somewhat terrifying when I realized I was my own worst enemy. On that note, I'm willing to talk about it because I don't want depression or anxieties to be taboos anymore. I came out stronger and more compassionate. If you or anyone you know is struggling with depression, seek help. It is the best gift I ever gave myself.

LODESTONE
BOOKS

Lodestone Books is a new imprint, which offers a broad spectrum of subjects in YA/NA literature. Compelling reading, the Teen/Young/New Adult reader is sure to find something edgy, enticing and innovative. From dystopian societies, through a whole range of fantasy, horror, science fiction and paranormal fiction, all the way to the other end of the sphere, historical drama, steam-punk adventure, and everything in between. You'll find stories of crime, coming of age and contemporary romance. Whatever your preference you will discover it here.